Penny Sumner was born in A
to Britain as a postgraduate st
at Oxford. She now lives in N
she lectures in contemporary ....
University of Northumbria and edits the feminist
creative writing magazine, *Writing Women*.

The End of April is her first novel.

The End of April

A VICTORIA CROSS MYSTERY BY
PENNY SUMNER

Published in Great Britain by The Women's Press Ltd, 1993
A member of the Namara Group
34 Great Sutton Street, London EC1V 0DX

First published in the United States of America by
The Naiad Press, Inc, PO Box 10543, Tallahassee,
FL 32302, 1992

British Library Cataloguing-in-Publication Data
A catalogue record for this book is available from the
British Library

ISBN 0 7043 4358 4

Printed and bound in Great Britain by
BPCC Hazells Ltd
Member of BPCC Ltd

For Pamela

PART ONE

PART ONE

CHAPTER ONE

I was given three pieces of advice when I joined the agency. 1) Don't take on a job if the client suggests you carry a gun. 2) Never work for a relative. 3) Don't get emotionally involved. Six years later I was about to break two out of three. I knew from the start I was in breach of number two, but as I was being employed for my skills as an archivist, not a detective, I told myself it didn't count. No one came up with the idea I should carry hardware, so number one wasn't a problem, which leaves number three, emotional involvement. I fell in love.

Arriving back in England I wasn't expecting grand passion — that was just one of fate's little surprises. However if it really was fate that brought me and April together, then Rosemary gets to play one of the gnarled sisters, and gnarled isn't the word I'd use to describe my great aunt. Rosemary is well-groomed, manicured even, her hands elegant and white against the tweed and navy of her suits. She looks more like a successful businesswoman than a don and her offer of a temporary part-time job was made with an efficiency I've only infrequently come across in the various academics who've hired my services. She laid out her proposal in a brief transatlantic call and I was impressed and grateful at the same time, though she didn't seem to think the latter was particularly necessary.

"It suits both of us. I know you can do the work and I thought you might like a few weeks acclimatizing before plunging back into London life."

As usual, she was right. Three weeks later I'd left New York for Oxford.

Rosemary raised her eyes about something that was being said on the other end of the phone and I returned to her well-stocked bookshelves. I couldn't see anything I'd rush to borrow, but I could see a number of items that would be worth someone's while lifting. She put the receiver down as I gently turned the vellum leaves of a particularly choice-looking piece of incunabula.

4

I said, "I hope you've got this lot properly insured."

She sighed. "So do I, but it's difficult putting a price on that sort of thing."

Automatically I did a quick survey of her office. "Is there a decent lock on the door? Does everything shut securely?" Catching her look I winced for myself; given half a chance I'd be checking for phone-taps.

"I let it be known I was leaving my library to the College and the next morning the Bursar was in here, personally screwing bolts onto all the window frames."

"Bolts! You know there are much more effective . . ."

She shook her head and laughed out loud. "Victoria, have I hired myself an archivist or a private detective?"

I laughed too. "Conan the Librarian at your service, ma'am."

Where Rosemary's room was wall-to-wall bookcases and surfaces piled with neat stacks of paper, her neighbor's office looked suspiciously bare.

"You're sure he's just on sabbatical? It looks to me like he's cleared out for good."

She sat down in front of a microfilm reader and began threading a thin ribbon of film from one grey spool to another. "He claims he's in the States to attend a conference on 'Popular Culture and Postmodernism' but I suspect it's actually one of those dreadful events where one touts for interviews."

I'd heard about them. "Known in the trade as cattle markets."

"Precisely." She leaned back and started turning

one of the handles. "I've purloined this from the College library. I do hope it's working properly, I'd hate you to end up with eyesight like mine."

As the film squeaked across the lens I peered over her shoulder. With antiquated equipment like this I could sympathize with the postmodernist. "Looks readable." Just.

"Right, I'll wind it through to the first manuscript. If you're interested, you'll find a copy of my research proposal on top of those papers."

Jetlagged on a Monday morning, I'd have been a lot more interested in locating a cup of strong coffee, but as that didn't appear to be an immediate possibility I dutifully picked up the proposal. It didn't take much to realize that adding in all the bits meant to be read between the lines would have expanded it into three sheets of A4-size paper rather than one. It also didn't take much to work out why she'd been uncharacteristically vague about the sort of material I'd actually be working on.

Maybe this was an April Fool's joke, but I didn't think so. "You didn't write this for your publisher did you?"

She gave me a quick glance and chuckled. "Good heavens no. What you're reading was carefully constructed for the College committee that gave me the grant to employ you. I had to word it so as not to frighten off the bureaucrats, or the scientists."

Lopsided handwriting lurched alarmingly across the screen and I hastily looked back to her neatly typed page while she fiddled with the focus. "Who was this John Llewelyn anyway?"

"No one special. He just happened to have a

private income which allowed him to build up a fairly comprehensive collection ..."

"... of, to quote your proposal, 'illicit sexual writing of the late nineteenth century.' Euphemism aside, can I take it I'm right in thinking you're employing me to sit here for four hours a day in order to transcribe Victorian porn?"

Although my great aunt had the grace to look slightly uncomfortable, it lasted only a second, which didn't surprise me. Dr. Rosemary Myers had built her reputation on an ability to treat controversial topics with a clinical intelligence and, according to her critics, ruthless detachment.

"In recent years there have been a number of general, and I must say superficial, discussions of nineteenth-century pornography; what I want to do is look at the industry as a whole — writers, retailers, buyers. The manuscripts you'll be transcribing were rare pieces copied out by hand by Llewelyn and circulated privately amongst his friends. It really is very unusual source material. One famous collector of the time was reported as saying he'd commit murder to get his hands on some of these texts."

"I'll bet."

From where I stood the lawn outside was a chessboard of green; from the distance came a faint peal of church bells. I gazed out at the view and found myself wondering yet again why people never believe me when I say I've worked on weirder assignments as an archivist than as a private detective.

I spent the rest of the morning working on the

microfilm, then put the spools back in their labeled boxes and insisted Rosemary escort me to Hall for lunch. The previous night it had rained but today predicted an unusually vernal April. The sky was a brilliant blue and there were mauve and yellow pansies in the window boxes and a scattering of undergraduates on the grass. As we skirted St. Frideswide's central quad I scrutinized the students enviously.

"Is it my imagination or are they all remarkably attractive?"

She didn't bother to look. "When I was an undergraduate I thought it was because the rest of them had a great deal more money than I. Now I put it down to youth."

I decided to go with the money theory. To my aging eyes anything under the age of twenty-five looked squeaky clean, and that thought left me feeling decidedly anxious.

A discreet side door opened onto the clash of cutlery and raised voices. I asked, "Would you prefer me not to say too much about what we're working on?"

Rosemary took my elbow and ushered me forward. "My dear, I can assure you that none of my distinguished colleagues would dream of expressing any interest at all in what we're doing ..."

She was right; down our end of the table the conversation centered on the weather and the food, down the other there was an animated discussion about American football.

We'd arrived late and I'd had to take a seat facing out into the body of the room. When they said

8

High Table here they really meant it. The dons perched ludicrously on a stage while the students sat in relative comfort below. I thanked heaven I was wearing leggings. Concentrating on my plateful of salad would have been difficult with all those bright young things staring up my skirt.

Coffee was served in the Senior Common Room where the portraits on the walls all had thin wires in evidence, just in case any of the students hit on the idea of financing their stint on the proceeds of a Victorian dignitary. The furniture was of the same vintage and obviously kept on a strict diet of beeswax, and from the look of the upholstery it also had its own account at Liberty's. My inspection of the green flocked wallpaper was interrupted by a tall, grey-haired man who I recognized as one of the loudest of the Superbowl enthusiasts.

"I'm the Principal, and you must be Miss Cross?"

I could tell from the cut of his suit that there was no point in preferring Ms, so I simply nodded to that and to his offer of sugar. I almost opted for cream too then thought better of it. All those lithe bodies out on the lawn ...

"I trust you're finding your researches interesting?" I guessed the slow wink that accompanied this was to let me know that here was someone who'd had no problem reading between the lines of Rosemary's proposal.

"Tell me." He seemed to have moved a step closer without my noticing. "What do *you* think the difference is between erotica and pornography?"

It was a question Rosemary and I had tackled only half an hour earlier, but it wasn't a question I

9

felt inclined to debate with him. The appearance of a harassed-looking secretary saved me from having to offend Rosemary's boss on my first day.

As he followed her from the room his parting look oozed regret while I managed a cool nod; as he disappeared out the door a voice quietly murmured into my left ear, "Never let him get you in a corner, he'll slime all over you."

She was on the way to becoming plump, dark-haired and about thirty, a year or so younger than I. "Hello, I'm Phoebe Young. Dr. Myers sent me over to save you from a fate worse than being bored to death."

"I'm Tor Cross. He's like that with everyone, I take it?"

"Our Bernard's like that with every woman under fifty, yes. Roll on menopause say I — half my time here is spent ducking into doorways. I've got to the stage where I can recognize his predatory step from a hundred yards."

"Why don't you tell him to piss off?" From our brief acquaintance Phoebe didn't strike me as the shy type.

"You archivists must certainly have an easy life! I want a job. And —" She lowered her voice even further, "academic jobs being like gold dust, I don't intend offending anyone, especially not the Principal." She ran a hand through her spiky hair and gave a winning grin. She didn't need to, I liked her already.

"So if you haven't got a job you must be a student?"

"A student in the Senior Common Room? Never happen! I'm on a two-year JRF — that's Junior

Research Fellow, *Junior* being the operative word."
Despite the grin her tone was bitter.

"And you think there is a chance of getting a post here?"

She shrugged. "I have to admit it's unlikely. In fact something might be coming up, but my problem now is I've lost my novelty value. Principal will either want a new backside to pat or, if he's feeling particularly responsible, will decide a real job should go to some promising young man."

"So much," I commiserated, "for life in Wonderland."

CHAPTER TWO

As a child I'd never thought Alice had such a great time of it — tumbling into alternative worlds wasn't my idea of fun. How was it then, that at thirty years of age I'd dashed off to New York, forgetting how poor Alice feels shrunk down to a tenth her size? The answer of course is love. Love lost, in this case.

I'd announced I was taking a year out and had bought my broken heart a ticket to the Big Apple, where I grabbed the first contract that came along: my gesture towards the French Foreign Legion.

Inevitably, the agency I signed up with turned out to be the kind that wants blood, not the blood of their clients, nor, necessarily, of the suspects, but of the staff. I'd signed in haste and when I eventually located a magnifying glass large enough to locate the small print I discovered I was committed to living within fifteen minutes of the office. In other words, most of my salary would go to a Manhattan rent. And apparently I'd also agreed that four nights out of seven were to be at the disposal of the company. You mightn't think there'd be much call for a paleographer at two in the morning, but you'd be surprised. Company fraud usually bores me rigid but as I refused to carry a gun, and as I also refused to do divorce work, I didn't have much of an option.

"She's telling us she won't handle divorces?" Given a crisis Simon automatically resorted to the third person. "I hire myself a handwriting expert, a 'Questioned Document Analyst' certified by Scotland Yard, no less, someone who'll be able to tell me who it is that's been writing the client's spouse love-letters, and I get told she doesn't *do* divorces?"

"Oh, I don't think that's a huge problem Simon." Brad was a whole lot brighter and, as is often the case, a whole lot nastier with it. "We don't need to waste Victoria's expertise on matrimonial work when there's so much fiddling going on in the market place." He'd grinned but I hadn't grinned back. A couple of weeks later we played it in reverse, me grinning and him looking sour as I let him know I didn't do men either.

* * * * *

13

It had been Alicia who'd wooed me out of the archives and into her London agency. I'd attracted publicity by doing some work for the police to prove that a dead woman's apparent suicide note had been written by her husband, and soon after Alicia had knocked on my door and requested help on a case. That had been six and a half years ago and I'd spent five of those years not only working for, but also living with, Alicia.

Three months after we split up I'd caught the plane to New York, and now I was giving the final lick to my wounds in a summerhouse at the bottom of an English garden. Early lilacs were just what I needed now. Outside, the windows were framed by purple buds, inside they had borders of books with foxed pages and mottled spines.

During my first week back in England I diligently compiled a list of friends who really should be contacted straight away, but the truth was I didn't yet feel able to come up with the stories that would inevitably be demanded about life in New York. It was still too recent, not a narrative yet. I was hoping Oxford's soft-focus might turn it into one.

I had spoken briefly to Alicia on my first night and we'd agreed I'd start again at the agency as soon as I'd finished with Rosemary's manuscripts. She had gone on to describe the case she was currently involved with and I had cradled the receiver in a damp palm and remembered what it had been like living with her and wondered what her experience of love was like now.

Love was something I found myself thinking about a lot, although I had to admit that I was fast approaching the stage where I'd settle for sex — a sentiment I soon discovered I shared with Phoebe Young. However, where my stint of celibacy had lasted, not counting one brief fling, for nigh on fifteen months, I doubted hers would make it to the full half year.

"True love?" Phoebe tipped her head back and stared up at an almost cloudless sky.

"Yes, do you believe in it?"

"You mean True Love as in mutual devotion, a meeting of like minds, complete compatibility, topped off with unflagging sexual passion, plus, of course, life-long fidelity?"

"Something like that." This was my second punting lesson and I was still having problems persuading the aluminum pole to leave the mud, which explained our painfully erratic process.

She lifted the brim of her straw hat and peered over her shoulder. "You having problems?"

"Nothing I can't handle." My left sleeve was already sodden and so were my jeans. I didn't need Phoebe's patronizing glance to know I was looking far from elegant.

"Glad to hear it."

To our right another punt skimmed past, a shirtless boy sporting an incipient tan and immaculate white trousers. A girl lounged in the front, making no effort to conceal long legs or the fact that she was dead impressed. I was pretty impressed too, though by his punting rather than his biceps.

It wasn't hard to see what impressed Phoebe.

15

"Stuff True Love, how about True Lust?" She brazenly turned to catch the back view. "I do appreciate a nice firm bum on a bloke. With that I wouldn't say no to a quick grope on the river bank. Who knows? Maybe it'd turn into the real thing."

"He's too young for you." I'd almost lost my grip on the pole and was feeling vaguely defeated. Phoebe had done all the hard work, punting us up here against the current, and now it looked as if she might finish up having to do the lot.

"Ageist. You know I thought I'd found true love last year. It was wonderful, it really was. He had a great body, a great sense of humor. He was a brilliant geologist." She shook her head. "You know why he left me? He left me for the biggest pair of tits I've ever seen."

Phoebe's weren't exactly meager. "You're kidding," I said.

"Nope, they were enormous. He'd always told me mine were perfect. You know how they tell you yours are just right, big but not *too* big?"

It wasn't something anyone was ever likely to tell me. I'd stopped pretending I needed a bra years back.

"Well, when he saw hers, his eyes almost popped — I know, I was there. I also know that they were twice as impressive when she was starkers — I walked in one afternoon and found them doing it on the Indian rug I'd given him for his birthday. She was on top and her boobs hung there like ripe melons, they really did. That was the first thing that came into my mind — ripe melons."

"What did you say?" I asked lamely. Big breasts

don't particularly excite me, but the scene she was describing was definitely disconcerting. I put it down to the physical exertion.

"I said, 'Oh, I'm sorry,' like *I* was the guilty party, and she said, 'I'm sorry too.' And she really was, you know. She was nice, I liked her a lot. She was a nice person, plus she had these tremendous breasts."

Although Phoebe didn't seem to be aware that we were completing a slow circle, I was painfully conscious that the branch I'd ducked five minutes earlier was heading for us again. Kneeling to let it pass, I decided enough was enough. "Okay if we sit here for a while? I wouldn't mind something to drink."

I jammed the pole against the side of the punt and gratefully sank onto a sopping cushion. The weather was perfect for this. The last couple of days had been disappointing, but as soon as I'd seen this morning's sky I'd rung Phoebe and arranged to meet at the Cherwell Boathouse.

She passed me some white wine in a paper cup and I toasted her and the river in general. "This is what I call civilized."

"*This* is, yes." Phoebe hated Oxford for all the right reasons, but I kept finding myself looking for something to defend.

"I know it's a bastion of racism, sexism and class oppression, but you must be able to get something out of it — contacts, for instance."

"The most contact I've made is with our dear Principal, falling over me at every opportunity." She laughed and threw some bread at a stray duck.

17

"Have I told you what to do in a complete emergency? If he ever gets you alone in the library one night?"

"Do tell." My emergency procedure would be a knee in the balls, but I realized Phoebe couldn't afford such a luxury.

"Ask him about his contribution to the Cold War. It's the only thing that interests him more than sexual harassment."

"There's no danger he'll feel encouraged to flaunt his old wounds?"

The solitary duck had become half a dozen. I handed Phoebe a piece of samosa to throw, but she apologetically popped it into her mouth. "I don't think they'd appreciate the curry." She returned to the Principal. "He likes to pretend he was in charge of MI5, but the truth is he wasn't a spy, merely a bureaucrat who clawed his way to the top of the Civil Service." She searched a bag for crumbs. "Anyway, enough of him, let's get back to your original question."

"Which was?" I sipped the wine and hoped she'd volunteer to propel us back home.

"The possibility of a happy romance. I've told you about Howard, who bruised my delicate soul and left me the embittered, randy woman you see before you. What about you, Tor, some lady done you wrong?"

I'd had no hesitation letting Phoebe know I was gay; what I hadn't told her was that I had any career other than that of archivist. Being laid back about a new friend's sexuality doesn't always mean you'll be happy to hear she's a private detective. If people can't imagine what lesbians actually do, they're even worse about the realities of my second

18

profession. They tend to suspect that you're going to start unearthing guilty secrets, or maybe steaming open their mail. Sometimes, of course, they're right.

"There was someone I broke up with before I went to the States. We worked together."

"I see. Well, things are going to change soon for you, Ms. Cross. You have the look of someone who's about to strike it lucky in love." She stood up to yank at the pole and I gingerly squeezed past and took my place in the bow.

"I hope you're right about that."

"I guarantee it."

I met April that night, thereby proving that, had she wanted, Phoebe could have given up on academia altogether and made her living at the end of a pier, shuffling tarot cards. Like any scrupulous fortuneteller, however, she only told me the good news. She didn't let on that I'd drawn the devil's card: she failed to mention the man with the knife. Maybe, in the scheme of things, death by violence is a small thing in comparison with True Love. But I have my doubts.

CHAPTER THREE

Phoebe and I parted company at the boathouse, she wandering off to the Bodleian Library while I trailed back to the word processor to start the mechanical task of typing in the week's transcriptions. I arrived home a couple of hours later to find preparations for this evening's sherry party well under way, with Rosemary putting cling film over bowls of olives and Eleanor scattering cheese crackers onto plates.

"Hello there." Eleanor smiled. Rosemary would be sixty in a couple of months, so that made Eleanor about forty-four, but with her short salt-and-pepper hair and well-cut suits she looked younger. As she continued describing the day's events to Rosemary I sat back and wondered how it was that my mother had never questioned domestic scenes like this, had never queried the relationship between Rosemary and the young woman who had come to live with her.

It wasn't tolerance on Ma's part, I knew that only too well. The simple truth must be that the suspicion her aunt was a lesbian had never crossed her mind. I'd waited till my late twenties before dropping my news, with the result that in the six months before her death we'd barely spoken. So much for wanting Ma to now the real me. All honesty had achieved was a mess of guilt and unfinished business.

"A penny for them." Eleanor raised her eyebrows interrogatively as Rosemary headed upstairs for a bath.

"I was a million miles away, Eleanor. Is there anything you want me to do?"

"There's really nothing to do, my dear. There are only nibbles to eat and the guests all realize they're expected to make their departures by seven-thirty. Rosemary and I will have done our duty and all will be well for another term. How about some coffee?"

"Yes, but I'll get it."

"It will have to be instant I'm afraid. We're out of the real thing. I'm going to Sainsbury's tomorrow, can you think of anything I should add to the list?"

They hadn't asked, but I mustn't forget to make a contribution. How much did board come to in England these days?

21

"Damn," Eleanor said. "I thought I'd brought my glasses down with me. Are they by the kettle?"

"Not that I can see."

She sighed. "I must have left them upstairs."

"Don't get up, I'm on my feet already. Are they in the bedroom or your study?"

She smiled her thanks. "In my study, I should think. Try my briefcase on the desk."

Eleanor's study was at the top of the stairs, a comfortable Edwardian room with sturdy bookshelves from floor to ceiling and two bay windows which allowed for maximum light. Behind the door the massive mahogany desk was littered with books and papers and a cream and red straw shopping basket, but no briefcase. Turning around I saw it on the table opposite, leaning against the word processor. I fumbled blind through its contents for a moment, then my fingers closed on what felt like a glasses case. As I pulled the case out a folded sheet of paper came with it, falling to the floor.

I'm often asked what prompted me to become an archivist and, in an emergency, can be relied on to keep up a good half hour of dinner party chat about the aesthetics of preserving the written word, the politics of access to information. The truth of the matter — and, let's face it, this also explains why I joined the agency — is that I'm a snoop. Leave a diary out while I'm around and there's a fifty-fifty chance I'll manage to restrain myself. I've learned the hard way that references to oneself are rarely flattering and that even your closest friends get stroppy when they discover you've been leafing through their innermost revelations. Letters are another matter, however, and more than once I've been told off in a bus queue for reading over a stranger's shoulder. A solitary piece of paper falling out of someone's bag is the sort of thing I read automatically. In normal circumstances it would turn out to be a reminder to collect the drycleaning, but these, although I wasn't aware of it at the time, were not normal circumstances.

The word that immediately caught my eye was "cunt," not a word I'd ever heard Eleanor use. It went on from there, "you must have cheated to get into Oxford in the first place. You're an intellectual fraud and soon everyone in Oxford will know it . . ."

"What is this?" I'd spoken out loud, oblivious until now of Eleanor's appearance in the doorway.

"This —" She advanced and gently but firmly pulled the paper from between my fingers, "is nothing for you to get worried about. I followed you up because I remembered I hadn't left my briefcase on the desk after all. You seem, however, to have found its contents without too much problem."

Outrage on her behalf allowed me to ignore her rebuke. "Eleanor, who's been sending you this rubbish?"

She held her hand out for her glasses. "Don't get carried away, my dear, this isn't meant for me. It's a rather tedious student prank which, as Dean, I have to deal with."

I was immensely relieved it wasn't Eleanor under attack; all the same I still felt sorry for the victim. "A rather nasty prank I'd say. Do you know who wrote it?"

She gave an odd, almost sly, smile. "Let's just say I have very few doubts as to the identity of the perpetrator. Believe me, Victoria, this is a minor

College matter, easily dealt with. It is confidential however, so I'd appreciate it if you didn't mention it to anyone else."

I was being told to mind my own business. Although I was privy to much college gossip from Rosemary and Eleanor, I also knew there was a great deal more that would never be allowed further than the green-papered walls of the Senior Common Room.

"After you." Eleanor stepped back and I hesitated, then resolved to put the matter out of my mind. Eleanor undoubtedly knew what she was doing, and, despite my natural curiosity, one thing my experience as a detective has taught me is that there's no point in interfering when it really doesn't concern you.

The light wool dress took the slight chill off the evening as I dutifully did the rounds of the garden, offering cheese and crackers to bearded dons and apprehensive postgraduates. Given the chance I would have escaped altogether, helped myself to half a plate of crisps and made off to the summerhouse to indulge in a little light reading. But that would not only have involved rudeness but some physical effort; a couple of the guests had brought their bicycles in through the back gate and thoughtfully leaned them against my front door.

Phoebe was also there, doing her bit with a tray of bottles and glasses. She'd told me that the first College party she'd been invited to she'd thought she was a bonafide guest; after five minutes someone had kindly put her right on that, taking her aside and explaining that it was "a little college custom" that Junior Research Fellows served the rest of the Senior Common Room. I was sure Eleanor and Rosemary wouldn't expect this service from her but she'd insisted she knew her place.

"What, no sweet?"

She scowled back.

"I'm only joking. Look, pack it in, Pheebes. I owe you for the punting so how about I take over?"

She thrust the tray at me. "Thank you sister. I spotted some talent a few minutes ago that I'd like to check out."

"I take it it's got a brilliant mind and a pert backside."

"I know nothing about the former as yet but the latter reminded me of a couple of peaches. Tor, even you might be tempted!"

Rosemary appeared at my elbow. "How's it going?"

"Fine, your guests all seem perfectly happy."

"Oh, these events are fairly foolproof. Come with me, Victoria, someone I've been wanting you to meet has just arrived."

From behind, all I could see was long blonde hair splayed across a black sweater. Then there was a peal of laughter followed by the announcement, "For me life began with divorce!" There was silence from the red-faced young man this was directed at and Rosemary took the opportunity to introduce us.

April Tate was a complete knockout and all I could come up with was a bland offering of either medium or dry.

"Do you have any sweet?"

What had been impossible five minutes ago now struck me as delightful. Her companion ran a nervous finger around his collar and hesitantly asked for orange juice, at which Rosemary whisked him off in the direction of the kitchen.

"Thank you," April said, although it was unclear whether she was thanking me for the Bristol Cream or for rescuing her from an unresponsive audience. "I've seen you around College, haven't I?"

And I hadn't seen her? I had to be developing glaucoma, or possibly a brain tumor. "I'm doing some research for Rosemary," I said. "And you?"

"I'm studying law." She looked vaguely disgruntled at the thought and stared down at the grass. I followed her gaze, discovering in the process that below the sweater she was wearing short red shorts over black leggings and yellow shoes. On her it was a combination of genius that left me searching for my next line.

"Isn't that unusual for a lawyer to be doing postgraduate work? I thought you all went off to earn heaps of money in the real world?" Scintillating dialogue this wasn't, but my mind seemed to be narrowing itself at a frightening rate. Right at that moment it didn't seem able to stretch any further than her slim hips.

"I'm not a postgraduate student, merely a humble second-year. I'm only included in the Middle Common Room because of my advanced age." A thin wire of tension played across her shoulders but she relaxed in a moment and allowed her mouth to fall into a faint smile.

She looked about twenty-seven, twenty-eight, and I found myself regretting that she wasn't a little advanced past that. Thirty would have been nice. As I abandoned the tray of sherry on a garden bench she bent to steady it and I couldn't help but notice how easily her breasts moved under the knitted cotton. Phoebe could have her peaches, I was mentally juggling apples and pears. April Tate mightn't yet have been an object of True Love, but she was already an object of desire.

As she straightened, I attempted to stifle the excitement that had my own breasts standing happily against my dress. I hadn't felt like this for ... well, not for a couple of months anyway. And that had only lasted while we were in the dimly-lit club, trading sips of martini and the play of damp fingers under the table. In the cab on the way back to Meg's Greenwich Village apartment I'd begun to realize it was all a dreadful mistake. The next morning I was ready to hate myself. On this fine spring evening I couldn't imagine hating either myself or April Tate in the morning.

"Any of that dry left?" Phoebe jiggled my elbow and nodded towards her companion. "This is Malcolm. He's from New Zealand." She giggled at that while Malcolm stooped slightly and held out his hand. I was still feeling dazed and wasn't sure if he wanted to shake or was expecting something to drink. I squeezed his fingers, just in case, then handed him a bottle and an empty glass. Phoebe continued, oblivious. "And this is Tor, and this is April." What followed was a re-run of the stories she'd entertained me with on our journey up the river in the morning. "Quaint Traditions at Oxford" she called them. Malcolm was obviously fascinated; so was I, but not by Phoebe's anecdotes.

". . . and at Balliol —" She wagged a finger in front of his nose, "you must remember never, never, to pull the bench out from under the dining table. You have to slide in. If you don't it's a dead giveaway that you haven't been to public school."

"They also piss against a wall, don't they?" April contributed. She smiled at me again. I smiled back.

"They do." Phoebe nodded sagely. "Once a year they line up and piss against a wall they share with Trinity. I forgot what the point of the exercise is supposed to be."

Malcolm said, "What about the women?"

Phoebe lost steam in the face of this query. "What do you mean?" she demanded.

Malcolm politely rephrased his question. "Do the women urinate against the wall too?"

"Of course they bloody don't!" she snapped. "They've got more sense! What we're talking about here is masculine traditions. Oxford, after all, *is* a masculine tradition."

The New Zealander looked chastened and listened carefully to the rest of the litany, which included orgies of destruction at Oriel after the annual boat race, snuff-taking after dinner at Christ Church, at which High Tables demanded the cutting of grapes with silver scissors or the eating of a banana with a knife and fork . . .

I took the opportunity of whispering to April, "Is all this true?"

"A lot of it is, I'm afraid to say." She smiled across the garden at Eleanor, who nodded back.

"Eleanor isn't one of your tutors, is she?"

April returned her attention to me. "Oh no. If

28

you're studying law that's it, you can't do any other subjects. I know Dr. Litton in her capacity of Dean. In fact she's been very kind to me. Last year I had huge problems living in College, the noise was really getting me down, but this term she found me a room in one of the College houses."

Her eyes were blue, sky blue, blue as water. They looked directly into mine and I was drowning and not bothering to wave. It felt good, a long, slow, loss of breath.

"That's right," Phoebe chirped in, "you got one of the H.C. boys' rooms, didn't you?"

"What's an H.C.?" Part of my mind had asked the same question but it took Malcolm to put it into words. The rest of my mental faculties were still dabbling with the color blue. The blue of forget-me-nots, the blue of birds' eggs — I was falling fast.

"High Cheekbones. The golden boys who form their own little tory cliques. One disappeared recently — Daddy whipped him off to the States. The rumor is he'd discovered that his son and heir was dealing on the side, supplementing his already generous private income with illegal substances. That right, April?"

"Something like that. I don't know the details. All I do know is that Dr. Litton said I could have his room and I jumped at the chance to move in the same day. It's not that big but it has French doors onto the garden and there's a lovely fireplace — not that I'm allowed to use it of course!" She laughed and in my imagination I contentedly curled up on the rug in front of the stone-cold grate.

Ten minutes later April was making leaving

noises, something about law reports she had to read, and I found myself helping her disentangle her bicycle from the lilac bush by the summerhouse.

"Beautiful, aren't they?" She leaned past me to smell the young flowers and I had to stop myself from inviting her to park outside my front door whenever she wanted.

A petal came away in her hand and she absent-mindedly rolled it between finger and thumb. "Do you have any free time during the day?"

"Yes, quite a lot." And the nights, I added mentally, my nights are *all* free.

"Because there are various meetings at College." The petal fluttered to the ground, leaving her fingers stained mauve. "There's a discussion about women and the media for example. Would you like to come along to that?"

"Yes, yes I would." I tried to sound both interested and casual at the same time. The result was slightly strangled but she didn't seem to notice.

"Good, I'll leave a note for you in Dr. Myers's pigeon hole."

I held the gate open for her and dived into her eyes once more before she disappeared along the back lane.

Malcolm and Phoebe were where I'd left them. Malcolm didn't seem to have done much damage to his sherry while Phoebe had finished hers and was still dealing out horror stories. "The one whose room April got," she said, gesturing with her empty glass in acknowledgment of my return, "belonged to the same dining society and they really surpassed themselves in crassness last year. Usually they go for the usual, you know, women mud-wrestlers or something equally tasteful. Well last year they hired a couple of street kids to fuck in public."

"Are you joking? Where did they do that?" Stained fingertips and cutaway shorts momentarily vanished from my mind.

Phoebe sighed, suddenly deflated. "They did it on the table, after the club had finished its end of term dinner. There were all these disgusting upper-class fools decked out in their evening suits and gowns, and after the port they called in these kids and paid them to do it on the table. Apparently it was considered most amusing."

The party petered out soon after and while Eleanor and Rosemary gently ushered the last of the guests out the front door I scoured the lawn for glasses and paper plates. Rosemary soon joined me and casually asked what I'd made of April. What I'd have liked to make of, or rather with, April Tate would have been more to the point, but I kept that to myself. "She seemed very nice." That sounded safe enough. I wasn't entirely sure if my great aunt would approve of my getting the hots for one of the students.

"I introduced you because I wanted your opinion." Rosemary held open a black garbage bag and I gratefully released my handful of plates. "I don't know her well but I like what I've seen of her too. Unfortunately her political activities, combined with problems she was having with accommodation last year, have incurred both the Bursar and the Principal's wrath. She's been labeled as a troublemaker, but in my experience interesting students usually do rub a few people the wrong way."

"She invited me to a women's meeting next week," I ventured, "so I'll probably go along, just to see what it's like."

Rosemary stopped to look at me in the half-light and after hesitating for a second, gave a brief nod. "That's probably a good idea." She added, as much to herself as to me, "I often think we're in too much of a hurry around here to brand students who don't conform as neurotics."

Neurotic wasn't a word I wanted to hear but it didn't worry me overmuch as April hadn't struck me as the neurotic type. At this moment I was high on having met her but I knew very well that it was extremely unlikely anything would happen. The woman was a divorcee, after all. Still ... I happily washed glasses to the memory of blue eyes and red, red shorts. When I went to bed later that night I drifted to sleep on a sea of blonde hair; from above Eleanor showered us with love letters, soft as petals.

CHAPTER FOUR

If I'd had time to work on my fantasies I would
have come up with chance meetings on the bank of
the Isis, or at a romantic table for two in a candlelit
restaurant. As it was, I ran into April at eleven
o'clock the next morning in the corridor outside the
College buttery.

"Hi there!" I turned to meet a shock of blonde
hair and a pair of large violet eyes. Violet, not blue
— how could I have thought blue was adequate?
"Are you here for morning coffee?" Could I be

imagining it or did her right hand really rest, albeit briefly, on my right arm?

"Yes," I managed, "I am. Or rather tea, the coffee here's pretty dreadful. How about you?"

"I think the tea's foul as well, I'll settle for orange juice. Let's get a move on before the masses arrive and grab all the seats."

I perched myself on a stool and watched as she rummaged through a large green shoulder bag. "Have you had a tutorial this morning?"

"No." She shook her head and continued searching. "What I've been doing is putting these up on the noticeboards." She half pulled out a pink and yellow poster then thrust it back in. "Here's what I was looking for. I saw Phoebe as I came in this morning, she told me what you've been working on with Dr. Myers and it occurred to me that this is something that might interest you more than the other meeting I told you about." She passed over a bright red printed leaflet.

Pornography is rape! Close the sex shop!

How Seventies, was the first thing I thought. Luckily I failed to say it.

"The official opening's on Wednesday."

"Hasn't Oxford already got a couple of sex shops? Opening another one — I mean, aren't they a bit dated?" Protesting about them also seemed a little out of fashion.

"Oh they're not calling it a sex shop, it's being marketed as an 'adult leisure' outlet, specializing in videos and magazines for the upper end of the market, all very Nineties. But we say porn is porn and it's important not to let people forget it. We're going to stage a demonstration outside."

"That will thrill the enterprising owners, I bet." I laughed. "They'll be threatening to sue for loss of revenue."

"I don't care what threats they come up with. I won't be frightened off!" The words burst out of her, the tension that had been there last night was back.

I looked at her closely. "Have they been trying to frighten you, April?"

"Why should they bother?" Her shoulders gradually relaxed and she grinned. "In fact the manager told me that the more 'ratbag ugly bra-burners' outside his shop the better, it'd make his customers appreciate his merchandise even more!"

He obviously hadn't been looking at April very carefully. I wondered how she'd dress for a demo; today she was in a minuscule blue skirt that I hadn't dared inspect too carefully. I'd avoided a close look at the loose black sweatshirt for the same reason, but a quick glance floorward added opaque black tights and blue ballet slippers to the ensemble. She looked comfortable and sure of herself. She also looked great. On anyone else I would have thought the beaded earrings hideous but on April they were perfection.

She intercepted my gaze. "They're fun aren't they? My ex-husband gave them to me for Christmas."

"So you're still in touch with him then?" Last night's comment about life beginning with divorce hadn't left me with the impression that she'd be on her ex-spouse's Christmas present list.

"Of course!" She sounded surprised at the suggestion of anything else. "His partner Jen and I are good friends, and of course Gareth's happiest when we're all together."

Fuck Gareth, is what I thought. "Lucky Gareth," is what I said.

She tossed her head back and let out a hoot that caught the interest of a table of undergraduates. "Gareth's my seven-year-old son! My ex-husband is Will. He and Jen have been living together for three years now and they've just had a baby girl, May."

April as mother. I shoved that news to one side for now. "Don't tell me — the next one will be called June."

"May's the name of Jen's mum, they're not working through the calendar."

This was a picture I could feel comfortable with, a civilized version of the extended family rather than a harem. The relief I felt was a clear indication of how I was feeling about other things too, about the way April was looking at me for instance.

I looked back. Today she appeared older than last night, the skin under her eyes crinkling into laughter lines. I hated to think what my face was up to and just hoped the cover-stick I'd acquired in Bloomingdale's a mere six weeks ago was doing its job.

"So you'll come to the demonstration then?"

"Sure will." Like it wasn't some years since I'd stopped making the effort.

"Good!" Her violet-blue eyes darted straight into mine, "And there's a women's dance on Saturday night, did you know about that?"

"No, I didn't," I lied. I'd seen the posters around but hadn't been keen on the idea of turning up alone.

"Well I'm going if you'd like to come. I could introduce you to a few people."

Introductions to other people weren't what I was hoping for but I didn't let that worry me. We got up from the table and in my imagination April Tate and I were dancing already. I waltzed her past the door to the Middle Common Room, past the stairs leading to the College library. We said goodbye outside the porter's lodge and I walked back to Rosemary's room in a reverie that made *Dirty Dancing* look like *The Red Shoes*. So it wasn't until I'd reached the first floor and passed a couple of noticeboards that I caught sight of one of April's pink and yellow posters. A pink and yellow poster advertising, in bold black letters, a new support group for gay parents.

At ten o'clock on Wednesday morning April was wearing jeans and a white T-shirt; so was I. I would have liked to have had the confidence to interpret this as a promise of compatibility but was too worried she might resent being seen as one half of a pair of aspiring Bobbsey twins.

Paranoia, one of my ongoing problems, didn't however appear to be one of hers. "Hey, I like that!" She fingered my sleeve appreciatively. I was hoping her fingers would find their way onto my arm.

"Fruit of the Loom." I attempted to play it New York trendy. "Bought it for six bucks from a street stall. And yours?" My hand hovered a few inches from her neckline but then lost courage. I waved it in the air for a second then gave up altogether.

37

"Three-fifty from Marks and Sparks."

"A quid from a jumble sale, and that includes the denim." A woman in a well-worn grey sweat-shirt and faded dungarees lightly rested her head on April's shoulder and shot me a look which told me she suspected I wouldn't like it. She was right, I didn't.

"Are you a law student too?" Something told me she wouldn't like that.

The tousled head shot up. "Not everyone in Oxford's a student you know, some of us actually live here."

April laughed. "Tor, meet Jo, who finished a degree in politics last year and now works in a printers' co-op down the road."

Jo scowled and sauntered off to greet a young black woman who was looking for a place to chain her bike.

"She's okay, really."

"I'm sure she is." I thought she was absolutely fine now that her attention was elsewhere.

"She takes things seriously, which is probably no bad thing."

"And you don't take things seriously? So that's why you spend your time plastering noticeboards with lesbian posters?" It was the closest I'd got but she didn't seem to notice.

"I spent too many years trying to be serious."

I hoped that didn't mean these days she was ruling out serious as in serious enough to go to bed, serious enough to get involved with someone like me, but before I could sound her out on any of that she was talking to a pale-faced student anxious about her first demonstration and I was left in danger of feeling decidedly jaded. Here, or somewhere very like it, was where I'd been, myself, as an undergraduate a decade and a half ago. Then it had seemed so clear-cut and easy — in a short time there'd be no need for the women's refuges, there'd be equality at work, porn would be a dead issue. In other words the battle would be won. The battle hadn't been won and yet I wasn't sure how much that bothered me, and that lack of conviction was worrying in itself. Maybe I was still reeling from the 1980s, the Thatcher years: maybe the fact that I wasn't itching to lob a brick through the shop's windows was a symptom of creeping post-feminism, that slow slide into ideological angst. Before I'd given that too much painful thought however, Jo was back.

"Time to spread the ranks ladies, the God Squad's arrived."

We already had a Christian contingent in the form of an elderly Quaker woman and her husband who'd been thoughtful enough to bring a supply of spring water which, they assured us, had been collected by themselves from a site they could guarantee was free of both pesticides and sewage. The Christians getting out of the dark blue Metro were a different breed entirely, the British equivalent of America's Moral Majority. The first placard unloaded featured the words PORNOGRAPHY and ABORTION in blood-red, six-inch capitals. The small print was a virulent green and though I couldn't work out the words at a distance I could guess the overall gist.

Beside me April groaned. "I could really do without this."

"Well, that's the danger isn't it? You come out on

the side of censorship and suddenly you find yourself in bed with the new right."

"Hard to imagine," she said drily.

Jo and another woman began to argue with a gaunt young man carrying a LIFE placard and as voices rose I suggested a strategic retreat. "Shall we make ourselves scarce until this calms down? I could do with a jolt of caffeine." I also wanted her to myself for a while.

From the cafe across the road it was the people protesting who looked like the problem, not the shop. "Does it bother you?" April asked the middle-aged woman on the register.

She shook her head as she rang up the amount. "I don't really mind to tell the truth. The manager's polite enough, came over and introduced himself last week. I expected some big bloke, all hairy chest and gold medallions, but he wasn't that sort at all. Looked more like a bank manager than a pimp, which is a sign of the times!" She chuckled and squeezed April's hand as she gave her the change. "I appreciate what you're trying to do, love, but I've seen it all before. Worked in a sandwich bar in Soho for fifteen years and believe me, that place over the road is nothing."

When we got back outside it was threatening to drizzle and there were two distinct groups of protestors, one energetically singing hymns. "Do you want to pack it in?" I eventually whispered as Jo and a red-haired young woman urged our side to drown out "Jesus Saves" with the Greenham "Spirit Song." I was worried I wouldn't remember the words.

April checked her watch. "I have to. I've got a lecture in an hour and some books to get from the library before then. I'm going to London tonight and can get some reading done on the train."

"So you'll be away tomorrow?" Shit, I'd been waiting for an opportunity to suggest lunch.

"And the next day, which is Gareth's birthday. Being a student-mother is bad enough, but being a lesbian as well! It's all guilt of course, in case he finds it hard to handle later on. I try to make sure I'm there for every big event, the school open days, the concerts, the visits to the dentist . . ."

"It must be hard." Although what had really been said had been said easily, as if it was something she assumed I knew anyway. I didn't look up from where I was pulling a sweater out of my bag; the smile that had taken over my face was undoubtedly uncool.

She was still talking. "I'll be back late Friday. Are you still on for the dance Saturday? We could meet you at St. Fride's lodge around nine."

"It's a date." I hoped to heaven it was and must have let something of that show as I finally looked up at her.

April's hair fell heavily as she put her head on one side and gave me a long stare. "Yes," she said evenly, "it is."

Which was more than enough.

We walked in a companionable silence to the corner, April wheeling her bike and me so pleased with the way things were going that I didn't notice as the car drew out from the road opposite and pulled close to the curb.

"Cunt! Stay home next time!"

April dropped her bike and jumped back so that the paint missed her clothes, splattering instead across the pavement and her feet. I swung round to check that she was okay, then looked back to see the white Ford Capri already taking the corner.

"Fuck it!" I snarled. "I missed the number!"

"The number?" She was staring in obvious bewilderment at the bright red stains.

"The car number. Hey, are you all right?"

Her face was white but she managed a short laugh. "My tutor's a sixty-year-old who's terrified of women. What do you think he'll make of these suspicious spots on my shoes? Those bastards have ruined them!"

I wanted to put my arms around her, instead I picked up her bike. "I don't suppose you recognized them?"

She shook her head. "Unfortunately not. We'd better go back and warn the others, in case they come back."

"I'll tell them, you go to the library." I watched her merge into the stream of traffic then retraced my steps. At the mention of red paint Jo immediately pointed to the anti-abortionists' signs but this was hotly denied by the hymn-singers. I doubted that they were involved. It was much more likely that while the front men of a sex shop might look like bank managers these days, the backup team hadn't changed that much.

CHAPTER FIVE

I spent the afternoon working on a particularly tricky manuscript and in the evening went for a walk in the University Parks with Rosemary and Eleanor. They wandered along arm-in-arm and I trailed behind in a romantic haze. I spent the next day in a similar state and so when the phone rang after dinner and it was Alicia asking me to come up on the Friday night for the weekend I didn't panic. Instead I said that would be great but I couldn't stay for the weekend because I was going out on Saturday night. To which she replied that she didn't have anything booked for the next afternoon, why didn't I come up early and we'd sit out on the Common if the weather allowed?

For five years Alicia and I had rented a flat in Camden. After we split up I bought a depressing one-bedroom flat in Hoxton but had only lived there for a month before putting it in the hands of a letting agency and leaving for the States. Meanwhile Alicia had done the unthinkable and moved south, to a first-floor flat overlooking Clapham Common.

It was overcast when I arrived so Alicia bustled around making tea and I silently took stock of the familiar furniture in the unfamiliar rooms and then did the polite thing and admired the view from the window. By dinnertime I'd succumbed to the Alicia charm, although that didn't stop me from cold-shouldering Paul when he arrived. After dinner he disappeared into the kitchen looking faintly bad-tempered while Alicia, true to form, carried on oblivious.

"You like it then?" She ran a hand through cropped auburn hair and looked at me anxiously.

"Yeah, I do. You've got the cheekbones for it."

"I think short hair suits you better than it does me, but I just don't seem to have the time these days. Guess I'm getting older."

I fought down the urge to suggest she'd better get a move on, menopause could strike at any moment. If Alicia wasn't pregnant by now I knew it wouldn't be for lack of trying. I looked over her shoulder into the mirror we'd bought together one

Sunday at Camden market. My brown hair hung about an inch below my shoulder line. I lifted the fringe off my forehead with the base of my wine glass. "Should I grow it out or not?"

"Let it grow a bit longer and then decide."

We were playing at sisters, which was probably the only way to play it. And to be honest I had to admit it was easier knowing it was a man in the kitchen doing the washing up, not another woman. My feelings toward Paul softened. "I should go and see if he needs any help."

"It's okay, Tor, really. Sit here and tell me about New York, not about the agency but about your social life. Gayle says she had a great time when she stayed with you."

"She did all the cooking which makes her the perfect guest as far as I'm concerned."

"She also told me," Alicia lowered her voice slightly, "she also told me that you were involved with a seriously nice lady. Someone named Meg?"

Gayle might be the perfect guest but she also had an extremely big mouth. "Meg was . . ." Did I really want to confess that Meg had been a brief mistake? And that there hadn't been anyone else? ". . . She was fun but wedded to a Manhattan lifestyle. Which was altogether too fast for me."

"Any chance she'll be coming over here to visit?"

I was saved from having to improvise by Paul, telling me Rosemary was on the phone.

This was the second noteworthy telephone conversation I'd had with my great aunt in just over a month. In the first she'd called on my expertise as an archivist. In the second she called on my experience as a private detective.

PART TWO

CHAPTER SIX

I spent the return journey from Alicia's
speculating as to how the various pieces slotted into
place: the letter in Eleanor's briefcase, April's
tension, Rosemary saying she particularly wanted us
to meet ... So much for coincidence. So much, too,
for Oxford's dreaming spires. Right now the glow off
the sandstone walls wasn't looking all that rosy.

It was just after midday when I arrived to find
Rosemary in the kitchen preparing an early lunch.
She retold the story and I ran through the main
points.

"You're positive April wasn't hurt?"

She nodded. "Yes. It seems he shoved her a few times but she didn't panic and he didn't touch her again."

She'd reassured me about this on the phone last night. I just needed to hear it again. "Okay, tell me if I've got this straight. April took a shortcut from the station along the canal. Does she always go that way?"

"I don't know, Victoria, although I do know a lot of students take that route if they're on foot. It's more difficult with a bicycle."

"I don't suppose she would have left her bike at the station when she went to London?"

"Good heavens no, a bicycle doesn't last the morning outside the station these days. I'm told they're loaded into vans and sold the same afternoon at London street stalls."

"And this skinhead ..." Is that how April had really described him? "He called her by name and told her to get out of Oxford ..."

I turned away to look out the window. On the grass near the summerhouse was a lone glass we'd missed after the party. "You know, what I don't understand is the secrecy. Why didn't you tell me any of this before?"

In the glass, her reflection shrugged wearily. "Because I've got used to the Oxford way of doing things. One doesn't make a fuss. College handles its own problems."

"Even threats against a student's life?"

"Yes, even that."

There was no point in pursuing it. "But now

you're seriously worried." I piled bread onto a plate and sat down at the table.

Rosemary pushed the butter toward me, then fixed her gaze at a point somewhere above the refrigerator. "Yes, although it's not my problem of course, it's something that Eleanor has to deal with as Dean."

Eleanor's response to all this was something else I couldn't understand. "Now tell me if I'm confused about this bit. April has been receiving threatening letters for some time ..."

"Since early on in the term. Camembert or Stilton?"

I shook my head and stuck to the point. "But Eleanor suspects she's been writing them to herself and she's lying about last night."

She busied herself opening a jar of chutney. "You must understand that we've had this sort of thing happen before. It's a hot-house environment here and I can think of a number of similar incidents over the years, students who've created fantasy worlds in which terrible things happen to them, or they've been told they have a fatal disease, that sort of thing. Just two years ago we had a postgraduate with a razor blade slash across his stomach that he later confessed was self-inflicted. It doesn't help April's case that she's so cool about the whole business. Eleanor says she didn't seem particularly upset when she rang last night, which might just mean she wasn't hysterical." She gave an unhappy glance towards the door. Eleanor was working upstairs and it was becoming obvious Rosemary hadn't told her she'd rung me last night.

"These letters, have you read them?" I didn't bother to add I'd had a glimpse of one myself.

"I've seen a few, Eleanor has them in her office. At first they were what you'd call poison pen letters, saying April was hated by all the other students and it was obvious she was going to fail so she might as well drop out now. But I believe that recently they've become more threatening, and that does worry me." She hesitated. "I assume you've come across this sort of thing —"

"In my professional capacity, yes, often. Luckily I've never received one myself. Usually someone gets a few and then they stop, it's a way for the writer to let off steam I guess — but even so, they can be extremely upsetting. What is worrying about this instance is that they haven't stopped, and now April has been physically threatened. If the skin isn't a coincidence then it suggests that there could be something pretty serious going on."

But for the life of me I couldn't imagine what. The cases I'd worked on that had escalated into violence had all involved business rivalry — or intense sexual jealousy. The former didn't seem likely, while the latter ... well, I hoped not.

"I see." If possible my great aunt looked even unhappier.

"Tell me, Rosemary," I said slowly, "do you know if Eleanor has any good reason to doubt April? Has she lied about things before?" Could someone with violet eyes be a pathological liar?

"No, I don't think so." She studied the table top for a second then gave a sad little smile. "You might as well know. The reason Eleanor is so dismissive of April Tate is because she's in love with her."

There were probably a couple of hundred things I could have said in reply to that. I chose one of the cruelest. "So is that the real reason you wanted my opinion about April?" I even managed to make it sound casual. "Sorry, Rosemary, but I don't do divorce work."

Ten minutes later Rosemary followed me out to the summerhouse.

"I know," she said, sitting next to me on the sofa bed, "that Eleanor and I are very important to you, and I'm sorry if you're disillusioned. But you must realize that we've been together over twenty years now, and Eleanor is much younger than I am. It's only to be expected that sometimes there'll be young women she finds she's attracted to. As far as I know she's only had one serious affair and that, in twenty years, is not a tragedy, it doesn't mean that our relationship is not a happy one. In fact I expect it follows the same pattern as most successful heterosexual marriages. And I expect that Eleanor's reaction to April's problems is also fairly typical. She's attracted to her and is bending over backwards to prove to herself that she's not."

"I'm sorry I said that about divorce."

"I know." She put her hand on mine. "Now tell me what you think we should do."

In fact there was nothing that could be done until I'd had the chance to talk to April. Rosemary gave me the number of the College house where she lived but when I rang, one of her housemates informed me that April had just walked out the

53

front door saying she was spending the day revising with her tutorial partner and she wouldn't be back till dinnertime. No, she didn't know who April's tutorial partner was and no, April hadn't left a contact number. All I could do was assume tonight's dance was still on.

Eleanor spent the day in her study writing a paper, and I helped Rosemary with the shopping. After supper I ran a bath, swirled mango oil into the water and settled back for a long soak. I finished by giving the can of shaving foam a shake and reaching up to the tiled window sill for the razor: feminism for the thirty-somethings, feeling relaxed enough to shave your legs. At eighteen I'd been going to change the world.

The problem of what to wear filled in some more time. I wanted April to look twice, more than twice. I held up a 1930s blue silk shift, slit from thigh to calf, but thought better of it. In the end I settled on a 1940s black short-sleeved top with a pattern of glass beads edging the neckline, and baggy black trousers that I could both cycle and dance in. I pulled my hair up into a black band and put gold studs into one earlobe and two gold sleepers into the other. Stopping halfway out the door I headed back to collect not only the cover-stick and mascara but also my toothbrush and toothpaste. Call me an optimist.

"Hey, that's amazing!" April came closer to admire my beadwork. She didn't look at all like a woman who'd been threatened a mere twenty-four hours ago, what she looked was wonderful in a pink shirt and matching tights. It would have been nice to be able to compliment her too but I was conscious of Jo leaning against the lodge wall, and where April was looking pleased to see me Jo was wearing the same expression she'd worn when we were first introduced. Below that she was clad in jeans and an enormous white shirt with lettering drawing attention to both breasts. The right breast announced *Dykes Do It Better* while the left read *Wild Women Surfers.*

Jo caught my look. "In case you're wondering," she drawled, "I don't surf but I *do* —"

"Give it a break, Jo." April bent down to unchain her bike. "Let's go to the ball."

The venue was Balliol. A *Wymmyn's Dance* sign was cellotaped to the far end of the porter's lodge and we followed its purple arrow along the edge of the main quad to where a green sign reading *Wymmyn Only* pointed in the direction of some narrow steps.

A short, ruddy-faced young man in a dinner suit stopped in mock amazement as Jo led the way. "My God, James," he squeaked to a similarly attired companion, "is that creature what is known as a 'wymmyn' do you think?"

Jo turned around to us and jumped up and down on the spot. "Mummy, Mummy, look! The fat penguin can speak! Is that what's known as a dick-head?"

As the two young men scowled and hurried on down the path, I had to admit it was hard to write Jo off completely.

* * * * *

"What do you want to drink?" April's fingers lingered on my wrist and I was relieved that in the half-light she wouldn't be able to see my cheeks flush.

She reappeared a couple of minutes later, clutching two clear plastic cups. "It was white wine or white wine I'm afraid."

"I'm sure it'll be fine." I wasn't so sure that I was: for a start I was the oldest person in the room. Hopefully April wouldn't want to dance for a while. It usually takes me a good half hour and a decent amount of alcohol before I've shed enough self-consciousness to make it onto the floor.

As the volume increased she leaned forward and yelled in my ear. "So what have you been doing since we last met?"

"I went to London too," I yelled back. "Just for last night." The mention of last night really didn't seem to faze her. How could she be so calm about things?

"Where in London did you stay?"

"Clapham."

"Will and Jen live in Battersea, right on the Park."

"Alicia and Paul overlook the Common."

"Alicia is your ex, right?"

"Right."

"Wanna dance?" She took the cup from my hand and led me onto the floor.

I hadn't enjoyed myself dancing so much in a long time. I danced with April, and then with a group of women, and then by myself and again with

April. I was hot and exhausted and satisfied and then the rhythm changed to something slow and we were surrounded by couples, their arms around each other. Over April's shoulder I could see Jo, gently kissing a short, pretty woman with a shaved head, their bodies swaying in time with the music. I looked back at April who looked at me and suddenly I was reaching out to draw her close ...

"Fucking bloody hell!" The crash of glass was followed by several screams. As the lights blinked on and the music stopped the tall woman who'd sworn hoisted something aloft. "Will you look at this!" Above her head she was holding a brick.

"Shit," April muttered. "Well there go this evening's proceeds." She sounded calm, but my hands made it to her shoulders and I felt her shaking.

The dancers straggled up the steps, a barefooted woman, who'd cut herself, holding onto her lover's arm. April went off with one of the organizers to inform the porter and locate some brooms and I found myself left behind to wait with Jo and her friend, who introduced herself as Blade. I found myself looking for a knife but there was none in evidence.

"Do you think it could be those two we met as we came in?" I asked Jo.

She grimaced and rested her chin against Blade's forehead. "Dunno. Could be any passing fascist I guess."

April appeared at the door carrying a broom and followed by an irate, elderly porter who appeared to be holding her personally responsible. We spent twenty minutes collecting shards of glass and then wandered out into Broad Street. As Jo and Blade said their goodbyes I nervously wondered what to do next. Should I suggest we have coffee somewhere?

"Do you feel like a cup of coffee?" April got there first. And then, "Jen gave me a cafetiere which I'd like to try out."

We were going back to her place.

She'd been right about her room being small but I liked it all the same. There were green art nouveau tiles around the fireplace and the grate held a luxuriant fern. A bright Mexican rug covered most of the faded carpet and on the mantlepiece was propped a selection of postcards and invitations. An embroidered shawl was draped over the back of the sofa, beside which a low bookcase was stacked with law textbooks and novels, the former mostly by men, the latter all by women. I assumed the full-length emerald curtains concealed the French doors. The opposite wall was dominated by an ornate, heavy-looking wardrobe and next to it there was a bed. A single bed.

April came back in, carrying a kettle. "Someone was in the bathroom so I had to go to the kitchen for water. Do you know how to use a cafetiere, by the way? I'm not sure when you're supposed to push the thingy down. Jen said to be careful and not to push it down too soon."

"No problem, I had one in New York."

She squatted to plug the kettle in then reached over and put a cassette in the player, asking at the same time if I liked a group I'd never heard of.

"You've been away for a year so you probably won't recognize them at all."

I sat on one end of the comfortable sofa and felt nervous and elated at the same time. As she spooned out the coffee her blonde hair hung down over her shoulders and she tossed it back as she looked over at me.

"Black or white?"

Blue, I thought, your eyes are the most wonderful blue. "White please."

"You take sugar don't you?"

"Half a teaspoon if you've got any, but don't worry if you haven't."

"I keep some raw sugar here for Jo."

"Oh." Well, blue-eyes, what am I supposed to make of that?

April answered my unspoken question. "Blade is her partner, they've been together for about a year now. Blade's only eighteen and was in a pretty bad way when Jo met her, living on the street and sleeping rough. I really think Jo might have saved her life."

Jo a married philanthropist, I was immensely happy for her. "April," I said, "why don't you come here?"

Her mouth was urgent on mine before moving down to my throat, my breast. "April," I heard myself saying, "please." Not knowing if that meant please undress or please don't stop or ... For some reason it no longer seemed to matter.

CHAPTER SEVEN

Two hours later and in the cafetiere the coffee was stone cold. She pushed against my shoulder. "It's your turn to fill the kettle. The bathroom is two doors down, on the right."

"And if it's occupied?"

"The kitchen's at the far end of the hall, on the left."

I fell out of bed and shrugged into her white toweling gown. "And if I meet one of your housemates?"

She yawned and pulled the duvet straight to cover her feet. "I guess you say hi. That's what I say to the various odd-bods I meet on their way to the loo in the middle of the night."

From behind the bathroom door came the sound of a running shower and two sets of giggles, one male, one female. I turned and padded along the hall to the kitchen which, unlike those I'd shared as a student, was immediately remarkable for being spotless. But then I'd never lived in a house which had a college scout come in to clean each weekday.

A young man in a dinner suit sat at the large wooden table, nursing a mug of coffee. "Hi," I said.

"Good evening." His accent was a thin layer of Oxford on a solid slab of Eton. There was no doubt about it, he'd been bred for those cheekbones.

"I've come to fill the kettle and to lay to rest some dead coffee."

"Please do." He pulled his chair in so I could get to the sink. "You're Tor Cross aren't you, a friend of April's?" Then, before I could answer, "You see, Watson, the lady in question had been pointed out to me in Hall, lunching with Dr. Myers. And how did I deduce she was a friend of Ms. Tate's? By the white dressing gown, which I had earlier in the week discussed with Ms. Tate, asking her where I could acquire such an item for my sister's birthday." His smile was warm, his brown eyes all boyish insecurity. "Do tell me I'm right and that I'm not just smashed and making a complete ass of myself."

What the hell, I was feeling generous. I bowed my head in acknowledgment. "Your deductions as to my identity are spot-on."

He stood up and solemnly bowed back. "Antony

at your service, ma'am. Here, let me turn on the tap."

"Thank you. You've been dining out?"

"Yes, for my sins. It was a rather dreary event I'm afraid, so I drank too much and left early. So here I sit, lovely lady, alone in the dark kitchen of the soul." His smile was wistful but his eyes were more knowing than before. "Little did I think that a woman in white would walk into my life ..."

"In search of water for her kettle. Good night, Antony."

"Good night!" The tone was reproachful. As I turned to close the door he kissed his hand at me.

"You didn't get lost?" The sight of April in bed and my heart gave a thud.

"I did not. There was an orgy going on in the bathroom so I went along to the kitchen, where I met a drunken young man who reminded me a little of the Andrex puppy, but with an upper-class accent."

"Did he also have auburn hair rising above his glorious forehead in one perfect wave, eyelashes you'd kill for and cheekbones you could cut yourself on?"

"If you let him get that close. His name is Antony."

"The house pretty boy. Hey, Tor ..."

"Mmm?" I was concentrating on spooning coffee into the cafetiere, but not concentrating so hard that my breathing didn't change at the tone that had crept into her voice.

"Come here."

"No way," I said in an effort at hard-to-get. "This coffee is going to get made."

* * * * *

I'd been right that evening amidst the lilacs. I
didn't wake up hating April Tate, I woke up in love
with her. Sliding out of the narrow bed I collected
the toothbrush and toothpaste from my bag, slipped
back into the dressing gown and, clutching the
kettle, headed for the bathroom. This time it was
empty. I filled the kettle, peed, cleaned my teeth and
prodded my fringe into something less quiff-like.

Back in the bedroom I looked at April asleep.
She wasn't neurotic, or a liar. She was sane and
intelligent and precious and someone was threatening
to hurt her.

"What are you thinking about?"

Not asleep, wrong again. "About where you might
keep tea bags, assuming your supplies run to tea
bags, that is."

She yawned and sat up. "They're in the cupboard
in front of you. I have lemon grass, Red Zinger,
camomile . . ."

"Any chance of bourgeois Earl Grey?"

"That too. Black coffee for me please, instant will
do."

I kissed her on the cheek as I handed her a
mug.

"Toothpaste! How did you manage to find that if
you couldn't locate the tea?"

"Oh, I just happened to be carrying a supply
with me . . ."

"Tor!" Her eyes were wide. "I thought last night
was spontaneous, unplanned passion."

"My Ma told me always to be prepared." But

somehow I didn't think this was what Ma had had in mind.

April went to the bathroom and I slowly got dressed. There were so many things I wanted to ask, maybe breakfast would provide an opportunity. She came back looking scrubbed and fully awake. I shook the yellow duvet into place. "Shall we go out and have breakfast somewhere? My treat." At which a sharp stab of panic went through my stomach. What if she said no? What if she didn't want as much from this as I did?

"Oh yes, let's go to Browns!"

The waitress was glossy and tanned to Californian standards: just looking at her you knew she deserved family-sized demands for blueberry muffins and pancakes drowning in maple syrup. Looking at us she obviously knew this wasn't what she was going to get; with a resigned air she tucked a professional tea towel into the back of her belt and scribbled down our orders, a Bloody Mary for me while April was more demure with a Betty Blue and two croissants.

"You're making me feel terribly decadent," I said.

"Some of us are still students, you know. I'll have to work flat out today to catch up on everything I missed last week."

So much for suggesting a long stroll through the park — not that it was park-strolling weather. But this did give me the opportunity to raise another subject. I breathed deep. "I didn't want to say anything about this before but I don't expect you got much done yesterday either, not after what happened on Friday night." The arrival of the Bloody Mary and bowl of coffee gave us something to fuss over while we avoided each other's eyes.

"Oh," she said, without looking at me.

I flashed a glance over at her then went back to playing with my stick of celery. "I'm sorry April, but I'd like to talk about it."

"Well I wouldn't!" Her voice softened immediately. "*I'm* sorry Tor, but I didn't know you knew. I didn't know anyone knew, I asked Dr. Litton not to tell people at College if she could help it."

"She didn't tell *people*, she told Rosemary, who told me. Rosemary also told me you've been getting threatening letters. Hey, April?"

She reluctantly looked up. "What?"

"You have some pretty strange admirers, don't you?" I blew her a bubblegum kiss.

"Oh I don't know." She reached over and calmly stole my celery. "I don't know if I'd call you strange. Weird maybe, but not strange ..."

Twenty minutes on the subject and I was clearly pushing things, but I did manage to clarify a few points. For starters she assured me there were no jealous rivals. Absolutely *none*. The letters had appeared out of the blue soon after the beginning of term, at the stage when she was becoming involved in both the gay parents' group and the protest against the sex shop. Apart from Eleanor, she'd only told Jo and as far as she knew no one else in any of the women's groups in Oxford had been threatened in any way. The thug who'd hassled her was a skin, about twenty years old and with a bulldog tattooed on his forehead. She said he hadn't actually used her name although he claimed to know who she was. "I thought at first he was connected with the letters in some way, but I don't believe that now."

"Can you run that one past me again?"

She briefly shut her eyes. "I told Dr. Litton what happened because at the time it seemed there must be a link. But the more I think about it the crazier that sounds. I mean who would go that far? Dr. Litton as good as told me she thought I was being paranoid and she has a point — if I'm not careful I'll be seeing everything as part of some conspiracy aimed at me. Like that paint at the demonstration, and the brick last night — we both know those weren't aimed at particular individuals. I think that's what the letters are all about too, some nutter has got hold of my name and is venting his, or her, spleen against lesbians and feminists by hassling me."

She had almost recited it: April had obviously been thinking about this a lot and I couldn't blame her.

I tried a question but she jumped straight in. "You really are a librarian aren't you, every detail has to be accounted for! For the life of me I can't understand why you find this so fascinating. Enough already."

I pointed out that there's a difference between an archivist and a librarian, and then I led the conversation around to her family, her ex-husband and her parents. To have a hidden agenda wasn't strictly playing fair, but seemed justified under the circumstances. As we unchained our bikes all I could think of was that we hadn't arranged when to meet again. Would it be rushing things to suggest tonight?

She must have read my mind. "I've got loads of work to do today and tonight, but how about dinner at my place tomorrow? Around eight?"

It was more than okay, it was brilliant, it was wonderful ...

"And, Tor ..." She chastely kissed me on the cheek. "... don't forget to bring your toothbrush."

CHAPTER EIGHT

I changed my clothes in the summerhouse, hoping my hostesses had assumed I was having a lie-in. Which they had: as I walked into the living room Eleanor fondly bustled forward for a kiss. "My dear, I'm just on my way out. I must say you look better for a long sleep!"

Rosemary appeared a moment later. "Well," she said as she sank into an armchair, "no doubt you have lots to tell your great aunt."

After hearing what I wanted she sighed. "I'll see what I can do. I'll talk to Eleanor tonight or tomorrow and ask her to let you have a look at the letters. You're sure there's no point in going to the police?"

"No point at all, believe me."

"I do, and thank you for getting involved in this. By the way am I right —" She lifted her eyebrows apologetically, "— in suspecting that you're getting involved with April as well?"

"Yes, you are. Or at least I hope you are, it's early days. Look, I'm sorry if this upsets Eleanor ..." It upset me a bit, saying that.

"That's for us to worry about, not you, although I won't say much to her about your relationship with April yet. I must admit, however, that the possibility did occur to me the night of the party, I looked over and the two of you seemed to be deeply engrossed in my lilacs!"

Compiling a list of sources to check took ten minutes. I decided to start straight away, although Sundays usually prove fairly unprofitable as far as this sort of exercise is concerned.

I began by ringing directory information and asking for the numbers of Oxford's various gay groups. A bored-sounding Telecom worker gave me her version of the run-around before finally having to confess she did comprehend what I was after. She gave me three numbers. None answered. Next I contacted the Balliol lodge but was told that the porter on duty last night wouldn't be on duty again until Monday.

Which left Alicia.

"Can do," she replied to my request. "What did you say the ex-husband's name was again?"

"Will, William I guess. He runs an alternative

bookshop named Sacco and Vanzetti — uh, do you want me to spell that?"

"The Italian-American anarchists executed in Massachusetts in the late nineteen-twenties — I'm not entirely ignorant you know."

I myself hadn't known, April had had to explain.

"Anything else?" she asked.

I told her what other information I wanted then thanked her for her help.

"Don't mention it, as they say." She sounded almost shy. "Hey, Tor, you hooked on this lady or something?"

"Let's say severely interested." How about that? I didn't feel shy at all.

"But you haven't told her you're a private investigator?" Moving with the times, Alicia insists that she doesn't run a detective agency but a private investigation firm: the Yellow Pages, along with the general public, insists on the detective tag. Personally I don't care what title I work under as long as it isn't "private eye." I don't appreciate the implication that I'm a paid "voyeur" maybe because it's too close to the truth.

"I'll tell her when the time's right, but she's jittery enough at the moment, plus I suspect she won't take kindly to the idea of a privatized cop ... Which is how she'd see it," I added hastily.

"I see, well be careful, Tor, I have a feeling about this one."

I wasn't sure if her feeling was about April or the case, and I didn't ask.

Six postcards and two letters got written after lunch and then I tried ringing one of the gay groups again.

"Gay Aid, Sebastian answering."

For a moment all I could visualize was a large teddy bear. Did his parents now blame themselves? When I explained I was doing research into the harassment of gay groups and asked if I could meet one of the organizers Sebastian said he would be delighted to oblige. This, however, was only after I'd claimed to be chummy with one of the celebrity supporters of the Terrence Higgins Trust. The truth was that I'd met the guy once, but that was obviously once more than Sebastian.

"How about morning tea on Tuesday?" he asked. "I can't do tomorrow, I'm afraid, I've got a deadline for a review for the *Times Literary Supplement*, the bloody editor's been phoning me all week."

There was a silence here which suggested I was expected to be impressed. "Really?" was all I managed, but it was enough.

"Yes, he just won't take no for an answer. And on Tuesday afternoon I'm meeting my supervisor. So would elevenses suit you?"

Heck, I didn't have an editor in hot pursuit or a supervisor to meet. I said elevenses would be fine.

"Splendid," he replied, "that's simply splendid."

I put April's problems aside for the moment and at nine the next morning was stationed in front of the microfilm reader, wondering what on earth I was doing working on material like this, and what John Llewelyn had really been like. The manuscript I was currently transcribing had been copied out in 1890 and his letters of the same period were paeans of praise of libertinism: all very *fin de siècle*; I kept expecting Aubrey Beardsley to pop in for lunch. However, I knew from Rosemary that within two years our subject would marry a painfully conventional young woman named Margaret Lloyd, and that soon after the bride would be complaining in letters to her mother that "it wasn't a true marriage in the eyes of either Man or God." John couldn't get it up: so much for the revolution.

A few hours later I wandered over to Hall to be greeted by Phoebe. "Psst! I've kept you a seat." Her fellowship allowed her one free lunch a week and she could always be relied on to grab a seat that didn't face the audience. "Eating with the grownups, what fun!"

"Hush your mouth honey-child, you'll be heard."

"So?" She glared at her plate and speared a baby potato. A new lectureship had been announced, but it was to be in chemistry, not medieval history. She'd missed out.

"So how's Malcolm?" I regretted it as soon as I'd asked. What if Malcolm too had turned out to be a non-starter?

But her eyes lit up. "He's superb!"

I grinned in relief. "Peachy in fact?"

"Forget the fruit, Tor, this is serious, we're talking garden vegetables here."

"Spring carrots? How cute!"

She kicked me under the table. I kicked her back.

After my first College lunch I'd avoided the Senior Common Room but today agreed to keep Phoebe company. "Oh no," she groaned as we entered the Fellows' Garden, but it was too late.

"One for you and ..." The Principal's little bow he made in my direction revealed a definite bald spot. "... one for you."

"Thank you."

"They're lovely."

He beamed and offered us both an arm. Across his shoulders Phoebe's eyes were murderous. "Picking the wallflowers is against all the rules of course but if the *Principal* can't break the rules life would be dull, wouldn't it? Good heavens, this path isn't really designed for three abreast!" Chortling to himself he pulled us close against either flank.

Bernard's good humor continued for the next ten yards, reaching its climax as he squeezed us through a side door and into the corridor leading to the Senior Common Room. I wasn't going to let him pull the door routine again and was about to wriggle free, with force if necessary, when he abruptly released both of us.

Stepping forward he ripped a familiar pink and yellow poster off the noticeboard. "It's that bloody Tate woman, plastering the place with this muck! She knows that students are forbidden to tamper with the SCR noticeboard, she's done it to make a point." His voice transfixed a bespectacled mathematician, who'd just arrived and could merely blink back in bewilderment. "Well this is it, she's been nothing but trouble since she got here, corrupting the normal, decent students!"

As he stormed into the common room Phoebe pulled me around a corner. "What a pile of crap!" she exploded. A group of undergraduates sitting on the stairs collapsed into titters as she added, "Are you okay, Tor?"

"Me? I'm fine." And in fact I was, because although it was a long shot, I had another name to add to my list.

Half an hour later I chained my bike to a rail then squinted up the side street and along the main road, just in case a white Ford Capri happened to be parked nearby. A battered white Volkswagen was all I came up with.

On the door for the sex shop a handwritten sign indicated that the premises were open for business.

"Hi there!" The young woman behind the counter looked as if she'd just stepped out of an air-hostess grooming manual. She had a smile guaranteed to calm nerves at ten thousand feet. "Still a sunny Monday outside is it?"

"Yes, looks like it might hold up for a while." I smiled back before throwing a quick glance at the rest of the decor, which was up to the same streamlined standard as the staff. Where I'd unconsciously been expecting dim corners and a general seediness, it was all tasteful spotlighting and pile carpet.

"Don't be shy," she laughed. "Just have a look around."

"Thanks, I will." Though I wasn't looking for anything in particular, it was more the ambience of the place I was after.

The decor was subdued, but the videos displayed over two walls weren't, and after a quick look at a few of the more lurid titles I turned away to the third wall and its shelves of gadgets, some of which I couldn't figure out at all. The dildoes were at least comprehensible, coming in a number of sizes and with a range of attachments.

"... with knobs on!" She'd left the counter and giggled behind me. I half-turned and caught sight of a neat name tag pinned to her navy dress. Hi Stella-Ann, I said mentally before turning back to the display.

"Are these very popular?"

"Which one are you looking at in particular?"

"Uh, the one in front, with the bowler hat and the smiley face."

"Oh, Mr. Smiley!" She shook her head. "I don't know really, we've been open less than a week so it's hard to say what our biggest line is!" She giggled again.

I hoped she wouldn't suddenly recognize me from last week's demonstration, though it was unlikely — today I was wearing a cream-colored dress and my hair was loose. Plus I was wearing lipstick. I wasn't as turned-out as Stella-Ann of course, but I was hardly the stereotype of a stroppy feminist either.

"You sound as if you know what you're talking about," I just hate myself at times. "Does that make you the manager?

"Oh no." She was mildly horrified. "The boss is upstairs having lunch. It's company policy that a male employee must always be on the premises, in case of trouble." She managed to make it sound like a perk of the job.

I pulled a face. "I guess some of the customers might get unpleasant at times."

"The customers?" She recoiled at the suggestion. "It's the radicals we have to worry about, the feminist lesbians and the militants! They'd break all the windows if we gave them half a chance. Some shops have been firebombed, you know."

We shrugged in shared bemusement then I thoughtfully changed the topic to more pleasant things. "I think I might have seen your manager one morning, a man in a suit driving a white car?"

"It is nice, isn't it?" She winked. "Wouldn't we all like to be able to spend twenty grand!"

C'est la vie. Porn pays better than a Ford.

Now that I'd done the full tour, Stella-Ann was going into hard sell. "Are you looking for something in particular?"

"Uh, well actually I'm just getting some ideas for a present for my brother." I added weakly, "As a joke."

"I see," is what she came out with. That's what they all say, is what she meant.

There were footsteps from the back of the shop. "Good afternoon." His bank manager's smile didn't reach his eyes. "You know I couldn't help hearing your conversation while I was upstairs." He raised his eyebrows as he shrugged at his hapless assistant. "And I said to myself, that lady sounds like a journalist or something."

There was no point in hanging around to debate the issue. He'd got it wrong on the first guess but I had the strong impression that, given a second chance, he'd come close to identifying the "or something." This was a man with a professional interest in being able to spot a feminist lesbian — or even a lesbian feminist.

"*Ciao,*" is what I came out with. Go fuck yourself, is what I meant.

CHAPTER NINE

"I know where you've been!" She was wagging a finger at me before I'd time to say "coffee," let alone "please." "You've been spying, haven't you?"

"Let's just say I've been doing my homework."

She leaned on the counter. "So what's it like over there?" She nodded at a woman wiping off the tables. "Me and Brenda thought we'd go and have a look sometime, for a laugh."

I thought of Mr. Smiley with the bowler hat. "I don't think you're going to be terribly shocked."

"I'd take some shocking at my age, love. And I was right wasn't I, about him?"

"Absolutely, not a chest hair in sight," I deadpanned and she chuckled appreciatively.

After a cappuccino and a chat I asked for directions to the printers' co-op.

"There are two, the closest is to the right on the same side of the road. Halfway down the next block."

"Thanks. I hope you don't mind me asking something else, but have you seen a white Ford Capri around here recently?"

She shook her head. "Sorry love, I can't help you. One of your pals came over and asked me that the morning you were all here. Was it you who got the paint thrown at them?"

"It didn't hit me, just got my friend's shoes."

"Well that was lucky, wasn't it? It could have been anybody, you know, and to be honest with you I doubt they were sent by him over there. Not his style if you know what I mean."

I did know. I also wondered what his style was.

A bearded man in "Dot Matrix" said he thought there was someone named Jo who worked at the all-women cooperative about a hundred yards past the cafe on the left. I thanked him and retrieved my bike, wondering if Stella-Ann was watching through the designer Venetians.

Jo was behind the counter with the black woman I'd seen at the demonstration. She looked surprised to see me, and not at all enthusiastic, although she did manage a nod. "I'll be with you in a moment." She continued discussing art work with a harassed young man and I studied the samples pinned to the wall.

When she'd finished she wandered over, arms folded across her chest: she really didn't like me much at all. I found myself hoping the cappuccino had dealt with the lipstick, then pulled myself up. Why should I care what Jo thought about my credentials? And if I didn't care about that, why bother to pussyfoot around with the preliminaries?

"I've come to have a chat about April," I said. Her eyes looked amused and I silently added, "not *that* sort of chat sweetheart." Aloud I explained, "I'm worried about a few things that have happened recently."

The amused look was gone. "I see. Hey Ali, you mind if I take fifteen minutes?"

"No problem."

I followed Jo through the print room and out onto a tiny square where an old blanket was spread on the grass.

"Right," she said, "so what's on your mind?"

I was relying on Jo being concerned about April even if she didn't like the look of yours truly. I summarized events so far — the letters, the skinhead, then added the paint and brick incidents as possibilities as well.

"Yeah," she sighed and lay back on the blanket. "I wondered about that. I asked a few of the shopworkers if they knew anything about the car but no one could help."

"The woman who runs the cafe said someone had been making inquiries."

"So you asked too?" She looked over at me, interested.

"And I visited the sex shop this morning, just to get the feel of the place."

"Well well, quite the amateur detective!" But I could tell she approved.

"I've got some time to play with at the moment and I think this should be taken seriously, don't you?" This was the testing point.

She stared up at the sky for a minute then slowly sat up. "What is it you want me to do?"

She didn't like the idea of not mentioning anything to April but I won her over in the end on the simple grounds that April had enough to worry about already.

"Here's my aunt's number. You'll call tomorrow and leave a message if I'm not in?"

"I'll call, but remember I can't promise anything, it's not up to me."

We said a brief goodbye on the pavement outside the cooperative, but before I'd unchained the bike she reappeared waving a battered paperback. "Here, have this." She laughed as she tucked it into the cane basket then strode back into the shop. I didn't have time to thank her, but then thanks weren't entirely appropriate: a copy of *Five Red Herrings* could only be meant as an ironic disclaimer. But what the shit? Jo was almost as anxious as I was. She'd help me if she could.

I stopped at the corner of Little Clarendon Street for hand-made chocolates. Initially I'd been planning on a carton of strawberry sorbet but thought better of it, firstly on the grounds that April's kitchen mightn't run to spare freezer space, and then on the grounds that I'd have to put it in Rosemary and Eleanor's freezer for the afternoon and I didn't fancy explaining elaborate munchies.

No one else was home. In the kitchen I poured myself an orange juice then collected a couple of old cushions from the summerhouse and stretched out on the lawn with a pen and my list. I put a tick against Jo's name and added Bernard's with a vindictive flourish. Before I went out I'd ring Alicia and then Jan, a journalist friend in London. I'd visit the Balliol lodge, and go to April's via Oddbins Winery where I'd buy a good Vouvray. On paper everything was under control.

"You look pleased with yourself."

I squinted at Rosemary. "Can I offer you a cushion?"

She joined me and stretched out her legs. Despite the warm day she was wearing tights. "What did you think of the Principal's little outburst after lunch? I was most impressed by the speed of your disappearance."

"How long did he go on for?" I hadn't realized she was there.

"Oh, a good five minutes. Of course he clammed up very quickly when I informed him that the offending poster hadn't been put up by one of the students but by a member of the Senior Common Room."

"Good heavens, like Bernard I assumed it was April. I was going to warn her he was on the rampage."

"I expect it *was* April but I couldn't put up with his rantings any longer so I said I'd done it."

"Rosemary." I put my arm around her. "You are magnificent!"

"I was rather pleased with myself actually, I've never seen him look so disgusted."

"Just how homophobic is he? I mean, what does he make of you and Eleanor?"

"What do any of them make of us? Middle-aged lesbian dons are an Oxford tradition. I'm sure that's why it's always insisted that Eleanor and I attend the Gaudies and are there at dinners for old members of College. They do expect to see at least one grey-haired woman in a tweed jacket wearing a bow tie."

I kissed her cheek. "I've never seen you in a bow tie."

"No doubt I'm a great disappointment. As for Bernard, like some of my colleagues I expect he regards Eleanor and me as slightly pathetic but nothing to worry about."

"Well, great-aunt-of-mine, you've spoiled all that now by coming out as a radical dyke."

She pulled a face. "I've never liked that word, it's just an invitation for rather crude jokes about holes in walls. Now tell me, was your afternoon productive?"

"As productive as can be expected. Detection, like research, being ninety-nine percent slog and very little discovery. I've got a few calls to make before I go out for dinner."

"I told Eleanor you were dining with some of the students ..."

She looked vaguely unhappy acknowledging this half-truth and I hugged her again. "Sorry about all this."

"Don't be ridiculous, you have nothing to apologize for at all. By the way, Eleanor has agreed to show you the letters. I told her that you'd chatted to April about what's been going on and that it would be irresponsible not to take advantage of your expertise. I said you were interested in looking at the letters, I didn't say you were making any other inquiries." She stood up. "I'll do some weeding before I go back in. Why don't you go and use the telephone in my room? That way you won't be disturbed."

I took the hint. She wanted me to make my calls before Eleanor came home.

Jan, my journalist friend, had an answering machine that informed me that she was busy right at the moment but please leave a message. I said hello and gave her Rosemary's number. I then added that this wasn't purely a back-from-New-York call, could she contact me ASAP?

Alicia was in super-efficient mode. "Right," she said, "I've got the info you wanted. I got Andrea in the office to do a trawl on the husband and he's got a clean slate. In fact he and his lady friend are so right-on it makes me feel positively reactionary."

Fuck Mr. Wonderful, suddenly I was feeling annoyed. "Come on, Alicia, being ideologically correct doesn't mean a bloody thing. Look at the situation — this bloke's wife comes out as a lesbian, literally leaves him holding the baby, and then heads off to Oxford to become a lawyer. Shit! It would be surprising if he didn't want her to drop out or fail! He probably hates her guts!"

Alicia was unimpressed. "Tor, he doesn't have anything to prove. We're not talking beards and woolly hats here, this guy's six-four, good-looking, a marathon runner. The circles he moves in it's *cool* to have your wife run away to join the lesbians!"

The circles I move in it's not so cool to have your lover run away to get married and start having babies. I could have pointed this out but didn't. What I did do was try to clear my mind of April's ex. "Did you manage to come up with anything on the porn merchant?"

"Completely respectable and — before you jump down the phone at me — by respectable I mean just that. A businessman, no trouble with the law. This guy's been with the company since leaving school, he's experienced in setting up new outlets and he's been through it all before with local councils and protest groups. There haven't been any complaints I could find of intimidation or harassment. No reports of anyone else having paint, or any other substances, thrown at them. The paint-throwers mightn't have anything to do with the shop you know, they could just have been a couple of local lads looking for a spot of bother."

A pot of paint here, a brick there. "Yeah." I no longer felt pissed off, just dispirited.

"In fact, I remembered last night that I'd been to one of those shops, that same chain had a branch in Soho a couple of years ago. The emphasis was on it being a class establishment."

A couple of years ago Alicia had still been living with me and I couldn't remember any stories about this particular visit. I managed to chuckle. "Alicia, I'm shocked! What on earth were you doing in a sex shop?" Was it my imagination or did she hesitate?

"Oh, I was just looking for a joke present, for Fran."

Her younger sister. "Really," I said, "I see."

CHAPTER TEN

The blue silk dress would be fine for tonight but I'd need the black jacket for the bicycle ride. I folded some clothes for tomorrow morning into my shoulder bag; later I'd add the all-important toothbrush. I then spent a leisurely hour in the bath, radio on full blast, conditioner in my hair and Dead-Sea mud on my face. I rinsed the lot off with the hand-shower, shaved my legs and rinsed again.

On the way out I poked my head into the living room where Eleanor and Rosemary were having a pre-dinner drink. "Ladies, I've vacated the bathroom."

"Can I pour you a g-and-t, Victoria?" Rosemary made as if to get up.

I waved her down. "No, thank you, I'm cycling."

"It's nice to see someone in your family showing a modicum of sense." Eleanor looked, and sounded, annoyed.

"Rosemary been drink-driving again has she?"

Rosemary smiled but Eleanor didn't seem to notice. "Has she told you what she did today? Announcing to the entire Senior Common Room that she'd put up some ridiculous poster? God knows what they're all saying about that tonight."

"I have a pretty good idea," Rosemary said drily.

Eleanor stared at her and then turned to me. "Rosemary has suggested that you have a look at the letters April Tate has left with me. I think it's a waste of time myself but you're welcome to see them, Victoria. I'm busy most of tomorrow but should be back at College around three."

I turned the conversation to the weather then made my escape. As I went out the back door there were raised voices. Halfway down the garden I heard a door slam.

The Balliol porter looked even more put out than he had on Saturday. This evening, however, it wasn't because of a broken window but because of a drunken student throwing up in the lodge. "I'm sorry about that, Miss, she missed you didn't she?"

By about an inch. Bloody charming. I commiserated wholeheartedly with him about the objectionable nature of some of his duties and then explained that I'd been at the dance and had come back to check if they'd discovered who'd thrown the brick.

He shook his head. Nobody knew who'd done it, but then they wouldn't say if they did know. Not, of course, that he could blame the lads really, being told they couldn't go to a dance. "Though for the life of me I can't see what people get out of dancing when they do dance together these days. You should have seen the way me and my missus used to tango! You young people don't know what you're missing out on, you really don't."

You young people. I liked it.

At April's place the girl who answered the door was named Deborah and the people sitting round the kitchen table were Jeremy, Frances and Philip, in that order. There were ten residents altogether but some ate at College and didn't spend much time in the house at all. Deborah breathlessly explained all this and April winked across the table as I handed her the wine.

"Thank you, I'll put it in the fridge. Fifteen minutes should do the pasta, time for a quick tour of the house and grounds."

The house was bigger than I'd thought. I hadn't seen a great deal of it on Saturday night and the next morning had barely given it a glance as we headed off to Brown's. Deborah led the way up three flights and proudly showed off her attic room with its sloping ceiling and view. In the distance I could make out Christ Church's Tom Tower, while immediately below were a magnificent copper beech and red current bushes under netting.

"The college gardener has a soft spot for us,"

April explained, indicating the new shrubs along the back fence and a well-established blackberry bush down one side. "And Deborah's sown wild flowers in the front garden."

Deborah flushed pink and chewed her fingernails in pleasure. I got the distinct feeling she didn't have an older sister at home. On the ground floor April's room, number thirteen, was the only bedroom. Deborah solemnly informed me that the rooms were initially allocated by ballot and last year a finalist had turned April's room down on the grounds it was an unlucky number. Deborah didn't worry about the number thirteen at all.

"Me neither." April tapped her chest. "Thirteen's lucky in my family, my parents met on the thirteenth and were married on the thirteenth, two months later. After I moved in Antony offered to swap, but I said no way."

"Golly!" Deborah was readily impressed. "His room's the biggest in the house."

"He coveted my French doors and, of course, the fact that I haven't got any neighbors. He has problems with his sound levels and would be happier in a room where he could blast himself into oblivion whenever he wants. I'm afraid I was very mean and opted for no neighbors myself."

April's room was one half of what had originally been a large drawing room. The other half now housed a solid old bookcase, desolate with only a shelf of tattered rejects from the College library, and two tables with a couple of word processors and printers. Further along the hall was a living room furnished with a comfortable sofa, some winged armchairs, and a color television.

"So," said April, "what do you think of our humble abode?"

"I think it's great, I adore old houses that are just begging for a healthy game of Murder in the Dark."

"It was quite grand once." April ushered us back into the entrance hall. "It must feel it's fallen on hard times."

I noted that the plaster cornices had had a recent lick of magnolia and the parquet floor was lovingly polished. Times could be a lot worse.

"There's a telephone in there." Deborah helpfully pointed to a cupboard-sized room to the right of the front door. "We leave messages and letters on the table."

There was a large open book on the gleaming oak table and I wandered over to have a look. "A visitor's book?"

"Sort of!" April laughed. "We're meant to write in the names of any 'guests' who stay overnight, supposedly because of fire regulations."

I glanced at the left column but couldn't see any names down for Saturday night. On the right of the page a couple of names were "out," one had "Sunday lunchtime" scrawled after it, the other stated "Monday p.m. — maybe."

April looked over my shoulder. "Nobody puts anything in the book about who stays overnight, we voted not to, but we do tend to say if we're going to be away and when we're going to come back in case anyone calls."

I flipped the page and looked at last week's entries. April's name was down as away for

Thursday, rather than Wednesday, with "back Friday night, 8 or 9 train," written neatly alongside.

She said in a stage whisper, "It's against the rules to take off for two consecutive days during full term without asking."

Deborah chipped in, "As undergraduates we aren't allowed to live further than two miles from Carfax. Postgraduates can live twelve miles from the center, so they get to find cheap places in villages. It's not fair, is it?"

"It's medieval." April herded us toward the kitchen. "I've got a Canadian friend who was hauled up by the Principal of his college because he got married without formally asking permission!"

The others contributed with similar stories and I watched April deal with the pasta and thought about the book out there on the table. Well, that was one less question I was going to have to squeeze in, I now knew that anyone in College could have known when she was coming back to Oxford on Friday night. The field was wide open.

"Like the dress."

"Thank you."

"Blue's your color."

I resisted saying something stupidly sentimental, but only for about two seconds. "Maybe that's why I love your eyes so much." In the candlelight they weren't blue, or violet, but black.

"Thank *you*." She bobbed her head in acknowledgment and passed over the vinaigrette.

"I'm glad we're eating here, and not in the kitchen." Here was April's floor.

"I always find it romantic eating off a dusty carpet."

"I see, so you do this often?" Jo and her cache of raw sugar, but Jo had Blade ...

"No, I don't. What other questions have you got lined up for me, Tor?" But she was smiling.

"Lots and lots."

"Fire away."

"Mmmm ..." I lifted a fork of pasta, gave an expert flick of the wrist and lost the lot. "Marriage, I guess — I want to ask you about that."

"I got married because I was pregnant. And I was pregnant because I was sleeping with a man, and I was sleeping with a man because anything else was unthinkable. How about you?"

"I'd been thinking the unthinkable since I was ten years old."

"No boyfriends at thirteen?"

Oh yes, there'd been boyfriends but ... I shrugged.

"And Alicia? What's her story?"

"Alicia's bisexual and claims that's what we'd all be in a perfect world. Maybe she's right, who knows? All I do know for sure is that she fell out of love with me and soon after fell in love with Paul. She desperately wants a baby, but I don't think that was the prime reason."

"After this," April nodded toward the spread of cheese and fruit, "there's gooseberry mousse, and after that ..."

"Yes?"

"I'll lure you into my bed."

I'm ashamed to confess I blushed.

On Tuesday morning I sat on the edge of April's bed and handed her a mug of coffee. Her eyes were violet again, and I was more in love than ever.

She smiled at me. "What are you thinking about?"

About us, about the next forty or fifty years, about the slope of your left breast above the sheet.

"Mmm?" She nudged me with her knee. "You look pensive."

"I'm thinking."

Wait a month, wait two — this is what I say to myself.

To April I say, "I love you."

They all fall down, and Jill comes tumbling after. When are you going to learn not to rush things?

And then I hear her say, "I love you too." Just like that. "I've loved you since the lilacs. No that's not true, since before the lilacs, since the sweet sherry."

CHAPTER ELEVEN

It didn't take much to figure out why Sebastian, my source for the gay scene in Oxford, had chosen this particular meeting place, and it wasn't because of the *trompe l'oeil* backdrop. I didn't, however, fancy his chances: the young black waiter caught my eye and raised his, although it was hard to tell what exasperated him most, my companion's faffing over the menu or the fact that he was wearing a red sweater with Rupert Bear emblazoned across the front. I decided it was probably the sweater and winced in sympathy. It was pretty horrid.

Over chocolate cake and a pot of tea I quizzed Sebastian. He had stories about the rowdy elements in various colleges and discrimination on the part of individual dons, as well as a list of pubs into which he wouldn't venture for a pint. With his taste in knitwear I wasn't surprised. He hadn't, however, heard of anyone having a hate campaign directed specifically against him or her. After reassuring me on that point he asked about the man I'd claimed to be pally with, but I successfully fielded this with my own inquiry about his review for the *Times Literary Supplement*.

"Oh that." He spooned two sugars into his cup. "Yes, that will look quite jolly on my *curriculum vitae* won't it? A little something to mention to the Oxford University Press people next week."

As a conversation dropper this was wasted on me but I was feeling too good about the world not to play along. "You've written a book while still a postgraduate?"

Sebastian's brows knitted, but only briefly. "Well I'm in the *process* of writing one in that I've planned my thesis as a book all along, of course." Of course. No wonder Phoebe wanted to get out of the place. I ordered more cake as Sebastian continued, "I'm twelve months into the thesis now so it would be convenient to have an OUP contract to wave at the Yanks when I go over there for interview."

It was fairly disillusioning, I mean how could a Rupert Bear fan turn out to be so remorseless?

"You've got an interview in the States?"

He avoided my eyes and stirred his tea. "Well I haven't got an actual interview yet, but I have applied to Harvard and to Yale, which are the only

American institutions I'd consider, the others are really second rate by our standards you know. I'd be better off in the other place for a year or two than taking something less than first class in the States."

"The other place?"

Rupert Bear sagged despondently. Just who had he been taking tea with? "Cambridge."

"Oh right, I can see you wouldn't be in a hurry to go all the way up there."

Sebastian left, grandly announcing that his supervisor had invited him to lunch at High Table and I cycled the long way back home along the tow path. It was spring and I was in love. In love! I let out a whoop that sent a puntload of undergraduates into paroxysms of laughter — the old are so odd. Back in the summerhouse, however, I sobered slightly. Sebastian hadn't provided any useful information and I had nothing to add to my list. This afternoon I'd have a look at the letters and ring Jo. Now I'd try Jan again, just in case.

Much to my surprise she was in her office. "Hi there!" she chirped. "I got your message but it was two in the morning and I guessed by 'soon' you didn't mean at such an indecent hour. Though I don't really see why I should consider your finer feelings, Tor Cross. You only sent one lousy card from New York and I know you've been back here for weeks but haven't called."

"*Mea culpa,* I deserve that but then I've never claimed to be a brilliant correspondent."

"Levity before lunch — this must be a business call. I've only got a few minutes before I have to meet a bad-tempered photographer. What can I do for you?"

96

"What I want is some information about St. Frideswide's Principal ..."

"I do remember there was some talk when he landed Oxford because it obviously wasn't an academic appointment, they weren't after his ideas about Nietzsche or the state of the contemporary novel. Not that anyone in Oxford is interested in the contemporary novel anyway. When I did English we barely acknowledged that the twentieth century existed."

"I didn't realize you'd done your degree here."

"Somerville — how else would I have got my first job at the BBC? Now what is it you want to know about your man in particular?"

"Anything quirky I guess, but I'm most interested in finding out if he has any big hang-ups about homosexuality. Any stories about him having had it in for gay colleagues, stuff like that. His family too, he's married." I suddenly realized how wide I was fishing. "Oh, I don't know, maybe there was a first wife who left him for another woman. Maybe he's suspicious of his spouse now. I've heard he has two sons, I'd like to know if either of them is gay."

Jan sounded lukewarm. "What's up, Tor, he been giving you a bad time? Maybe he's a closet case himself, they're usually the worst."

"This mightn't have anything to do with homophobia at all. I'd also like to know if anyone he doesn't like has ever started getting hate letters."

This was more like it. Her voice took on a buzz. "He's been sending hate letters?"

"I have absolutely no proof, nor any real grounds for suspicion, so don't get excited. This is all completely confidential, okay? If there's anything in this for the press you'll be the first to know. Otherwise I'll owe you one."

The buzz turned into resignation. "Okay." We'd made a deal and would stick to it, as we had a number of times in the past. "I'll get back to you tomorrow or the day after. Now I must run, Harry'll be letting my tires down if I don't get there first."

Next I rang the printing co-op. An older-sounding woman answered and yelled for Jo.

"Look," Jo said, "I'm up to my elbows, so I'll just give you our address. Blade will be there from about four this afternoon."

"She will talk to me then? That's great, thank you."

"She doesn't know if she can help much, but she's willing to try."

I wrote down the address and said I'd aim to get there between five and six. Jo said she wouldn't be returning till eight at the earliest. Neither of us said this was a pity.

Eleanor's door had a note pinned to it saying she'd be back by three-thirty and would come to collect me. At her knock I began rewinding today's reel of film.

"Eleanor, this won't take long." I hadn't been alone with her since Rosemary's bombshell about Eleanor's feelings for April, and I was surprised at how uncomfortable I suddenly felt.

"Don't hurry, Victoria, I'm in no rush to get back

to my desk." She had a red and blue doctoral gown flung over one arm.

"What have you been dressing up for? I assumed you'd be spending the afternoon in Duke Humphrey's."

She snorted, "That will be the day when I can spend time in a reading room during term. No, I've just conducted an M.Litt, viva. A perfectly uninspired and threadbare thesis, but these days everyone's desperate to pass things because the number of completed theses a university can claim affects the number of grants it's allowed. Now I have to spend the rest of the afternoon chasing up problem students. The Principal had agreed to deal with a couple but now finds he's too busy. I suspect he finds such matters to be below his level of interest."

"And his main interest is?"

She grimaced. "Making the female office staff seriously unhappy."

The letters were a bucket of cold water; someone really hated April. There were eighteen of them. "There are eight weeks in Hilary Term, aren't there?" I asked.

Eleanor nodded.

Christ, how was April still in one piece? I carried them over to the window so I could study them in the light, and also so Eleanor wouldn't see quite how upset I was.

"Word-processing poison pen letters — what happened to reliable scissors and paste?" She thrust her gown into a cupboard and banged the door.

I breathed deep and attempted some objectivity. "I can't be entirely sure about this, but from the font and the quality of print this seems to have been written on a word processor like the one I've been using, an Amstrad."

"That's convenient isn't it? Nearly every house in Oxford has got one. We made a bulk purchase for College last year so all the students could have access to a word processor."

"You're right about word processors being common Oxford furniture but not everyone has the same make."

"I use one, your aunt uses one. What else can you tell me about the letters?"

"As far as the software goes, a standard template's been used, single spacing only. There's no way of telling what model machine it is, whether it's single or double disk drive for example."

"Would it be possible," she asked slowly, "to identify the actual machine the letters were written on?"

"Not the word processor, no, but there's a faint chance the printer could be identified. With a laser or daisy-wheel printer there's no way of telling that I know of, but I have heard of a comparison microscope being used to identify a dot matrix printer. There's sometimes a pin missing and the microscope can pick that up. And these are dot matrix so there's a chance."

She gave an ironic smile. "You'll be telling me off for handling them next. I suppose that's ruined any chances of taking fingerprints?"

"Not at all, although I'm willing to bet the writer uses gloves. It is a pity however that there aren't more envelopes ..." The few that had been kept were all stamped first-class and postmarked Oxford, which was interesting but didn't necessarily mean they weren't coming from outside the area.

"They've become more threatening," I observed aloud. A running commentary might keep my thinking clear. "And as they say in such cases, this isn't 'merely blind malignity — there's a method to it.' Somebody very much wants April to leave Oxford, the message is becoming more insistent that if she doesn't clear out she'll be hurt."

They were becoming more obscene as well. On the whole they insisted that everyone despised her and she was going to fail, but a couple that seemed more recent included graphic descriptions of sexual acts supposedly performed by lesbians. I doubted they could be performed by anyone. Without envelopes it was impossible to tell the exact chronology but the letters which appeared to have been written earlier in the term were on different-sized paper, eleven inch rather than the English version of A4, which is just over eleven and a half inches; and where the A4 sheets had perforated edges which could be torn off, the eleven inch sheets weren't perforated. I got out my notebook and jotted all this down.

"Well," she said when I'd finished, "I take it we're agreed that the writer is a very disturbed person."

"Yes," I said warily, sensing the direction she was headed, "but Rosemary has told me you believe April's been faking all this, and I don't agree with that."

"You can prove these don't come from her, can you?"

"No, but I have no reason to think April would be doing something like this ..."

"That's it," she cut in, "no reason. Not even April can come up with a reason as to why someone should be persecuting her like this. If we packed her off to the student counselors I've no doubt they'd be reporting straight back that we have a very complex young woman on our hands, suffering from guilt at the cavalier way she's treated her husband and her child."

I managed to keep my temper. "Have you told April that you don't believe her?"

"No I haven't, but if this goes on something will have to be done, I'll have to insist that she gets some professional help."

"And if she's not lying, Eleanor? If she really is in danger?"

"In danger from whom? In danger for what reason? Trust my judgment on this, I've been dealing with anxious students for a very long time now. April is a very pleasant young woman, but she's also in an extremely stressful situation and in my opinion is highly neurotic. I suggest you keep your distance and don't let her persuade you to become involved in all this. She hasn't been bothering you about it, has she?"

"Eleanor ..." I said, then stopped. The look on her face was pained. She didn't want to hear what I might say next. I took a breath and quietly went on, "April doesn't even like talking about this, but I'm fond of her." I gave this a gentle emphasis. "And I'm very worried about her."

She visibly flinched. "Oh well if it's like that ..." The sentence hung in mid air. When she spoke again she was brisk. "I'd be sorry to see you get hurt, Victoria. For your own sake I think you should keep away from April Tate. It's a good thing you're not going to be in Oxford too long."

It was only as I was cycling out of college that I allowed myself to go over the way in which Eleanor's words could be interpreted as a threat: there was the suggestion that I could be hurt, the emphasis on leaving Oxford. And what about the letter I'd seen at the house? Why had it been in her briefcase back then, and why hadn't I seen it with the others just now? Of course there could be a completely innocent explanation, or ... shit, that was enough. I refused to add Eleanor's name to the list.

The day had started off on a high but was fast turning sour. I hadn't thought of looking at a map and discovered I didn't know where Jo and Blade lived after all. The first man I asked sent me up a dead end while the second gave me clear directions then asked if I'd like a screw. "Go fuck yourself," I said and cycled off, managing at the same time to feel guilty for not thanking him.

It turned out that the address was closer into town than I'd thought, a turning only halfway along the Iffley Road. I rang the top doorbell with the boldly lettered label reading *Jo & Blade* and a minute or so later heard a window open overhead. Blade's shaved head emerged. "Hang on, here comes the key." It was tied to the end of a length of string.

The flat wasn't what I expected. There were the political posters, yes, but there were also embroidered runners, similar to those my mother used to use.

"Great aren't they?" Blade flopped into an armchair and indicated I should do the same. "Like Jo says, this stuff is authentic women's art."

"I guess so." I felt vaguely surprised, first at the idea, and then that I hadn't considered it before.

Blade had been a skin since she was twelve and found herself on the streets full-time at fourteen, the result of pulling a knife on her father.

"I told him if he didn't stop messing around with me I'd give it to him and he just laughed. So the next time he started I pulled this knife. I didn't have to cut him, he shat himself just looking at it. I walked out and never went back. Then it was the usual, you know, hand-to-mouth. I was out of it on glue in the middle of Cowley Road about three in the morning and along comes Jo."

"Has Jo told you what's been happening to April?"

She nodded. "Letters and stuff, she's told me about it before."

"And last Friday April was threatened by a skin who told her to get out of Oxford or she'd be hurt. It was pretty dark, but April thinks he had a bulldog tattooed on his forehead."

"Yeah, Jo told me. Fucking Nazi — not all the kids are like that."

"I was wondering if there was any way of finding out who he is. Are there many skins in Oxford these days?"

"I'm pretty sure he's not from here. I went down

to Bonn Square this morning and talked to some people and someone reckoned there's a bloke from London who has a bulldog tattoo. He sometimes comes to Oxford but nobody knows why or who he knows. They say he's real crazy."

"Do you know his name, and where he lives in London?"

She laughed and poured the tea into cracked wedgewood cups. "He fucking calls himself Prince, can you believe it? He spends a lot of time round Leicester Square. They say he does tricks, gross-out acts with businessmen, real sicko stuff. Some people are really weird, aren't they?"

"Yes," I had to agree. "They really are."

CHAPTER TWELVE

April was having a working dinner with her tutorial partner and we'd arranged that I'd arrive at the house around eight. If she wasn't home by then Deborah had a key to her room. I'd originally planned on eating with Rosemary and Eleanor but after leaving Blade I didn't feel I had the energy to cycle all the way to north Oxford and back. When I got to Broad Street I stopped and phoned Rosemary who sounded slightly relieved; at the same time I realized I was also quite happy not to be eating *à trois*.

Blackwell's was still open so I browsed among the books for half an hour and came up with a novel by an Australian woman I'd never heard of before. Then I wandered along Broad Street to the King's Arms where I ordered vegetarian curry, bought myself a glass of house white and, a chapter into the book, was fantasizing about how long it would take to save the fare to visit brother Tim in Melbourne. Two fares in fact. Tim is my only sibling, three years older than I. He married an Australian and we exchange occasional letters and Christmas cards. April and I could stay with Tim and then travel up the east coast to the tropics, where the novel was set. Palm trees, long stretches of hot sand, your lover naked in the waves, her breasts foam-flecked and golden ...

When I got to the house Deborah met me at the door, suitcase in hand.

"Hi there, Deborah, where are you off to?"

Even that was enough to turn her bright pink. She shook her head. "It's not me, this belongs to Frances. She wants her case left here so she doesn't wake everyone up in the morning. She's sprained her wrist rowing, so I offered to carry it down."

"If only all our happy family was so thoughtful." Auburn-haired Antony appeared at her right elbow and took the case from her. "Where do you want it to go?"

"Oh, Antony." Deborah reached out for it but he sidestepped. "Really, Frances said it can stay here by the door."

"Don't be ridiculous, darling, it might get nicked. Look, we'll put it in the phone room, that way it's not quite so obvious."

"Is she going away just for the weekend?" I asked. It was a large suitcase.

"Oh no, it's the vac! We're not supposed to leave yet, but because of her wrist her tutor said she could go early."

Jesus, the Easter vacation! What was April doing? Was she going away too?

"Just my luck." Antony gave a groan that won my attention. "Frances gets to leave early and I'm stuck here for the duration. I cannot understand why you and April insist on staying up, Debs. Oxford really is no fun at all during the vac, it's simply packed with language students. Carfax becomes a no-go area if you're over sixteen and can speak English."

I could have kissed him. "So why aren't you going away?" Which meant, of course, thank Christ April isn't going away.

He looked at his fingernails. "Because, dear lady, the good name of St. Frideswide's is at stake. In other words they're scared stiff I'm going to blow finals. Quite frankly so am I. My parents are out of the country at the moment so it was quietly suggested that it would be wise for me to stay in Oxford, chained to my books. Life, I am fast discovering, is immensely unfair."

Life, I thought, as he brushed gracefully against me, has done pretty well by you my friend.

While April shrugged out of a heavy sweater and into a lighter one I poured the wine and piled cookies and chocolates onto a plate. "So how come Deborah's staying here during the vacation?"

"Mmmm, thank you. Deborah gets to stay because the poor kid's an orphan, no family at all."

That figured. "And you?"

"I get to stay because I'm a mature student who's worried about the amount of work she has to do. The Bursar treats me as a special case, in fact after my complaints about accommodation last year she goes white whenever I walk into her office. I asked if I could stay and she said yes straight away and pushed me out the door. Which reminds me, I have heaps still to do for a nine o'clock tutorial tomorrow morning so how about you toddle back home and I join you there on the stroke of midnight?"

"At Rosemary and Eleanor's?"

"Well, in the summerhouse."

"April, I don't think ..."

"Oh come on, what I had in mind is that I could romantically tap on your window at midnight and then leave early. That would be okay, wouldn't it?"

It probably would, but what if Eleanor somehow found out? "I don't know, I mean there's a sink in the summerhouse and a kettle, but there isn't a bathroom April, there's no loo ..."

"So? I can pee at dawn in the bushes. It'll be just like Girl Guides. What do you say?"

What I didn't say was that, unlike nearly everyone else I know, I don't have particularly happy memories of Guides. Instead I said wonderful. I said amazing. I said I'd get another bottle of wine on the way home and would she please promise to leave some chocolates?

* * * * *

April did go outside to pee, and when she climbed back into bed I curled around her, her spine a crescent between my breasts, my arm between hers. Those letters, I said. She wriggled her cold bum against me in protest but I continued. Couldn't she think of anyone who could be responsible? She sighed loudly and I nibbled her neck before going on. What possible explanation had she been able to come up with?

She couldn't think of anyone. There was no explanation. She hadn't received any for almost a week now so maybe whoever it was had got tired of harassing her and had started on someone else. Couldn't I just forget about it?

And the skinhead? What about him?

April had an answer. She wasn't the only person in the world to have been frightened by a skin, that was their hobby, frightening people, they did it because they were frightened themselves.

And it was just a coincidence that he'd told her to get out of Oxford? It was a coincidence that what he said was so similar to the wording of the letters?

She raised her head from the pillow. "What do you know about the wording of the letters?"

"Rosemary told me," I lied smoothly.

She snuggled into the pillow again. "I don't want to discuss it now — I just want another hour's sleep."

* * * * *

That morning the postman delivered April a package. She didn't open it straight away, however, because we overslept and when she got back to her room she just had enough time to change and read over her tutorial notes. At least that's what she said later on. I suspect she was scared that the package came from the same person as the letters, which of course it did. April had a pub lunch with Phoebe and me and from there went on to a lecture. I went back to the microfilm reader and at four o'clock Rosemary came in to say April was on the phone and sounded a bit worried.

She said there was a strange package and I yelled not to open it.

She already had, she said, that's how she knew it was strange. It was stupid to be upset of course but there was a rat in it.

"A rat?"

"Yes. A white rat, with its head smashed in."

She wanted to get out of the house so we agreed to meet in the restaurant where I'd talked to Sebastian. I arrived before April, ordered a coffee from the same waiter, and pulled out my notebook. I'd heard from Jan — no go, she'd said. The only stories of harassment to do with St. Frideswide's Principal were strictly of a heterosexual nature. One Civil Service typist had resigned in tears. Conservative politics, no divorces, two sons both of whom were married with children.

"So?" I'd cut in.

There'd been a moment's silence. "So they might be as queer as coots," she replied, "but that would take some investigating. On the surface they're heterosexual and happy about it." She added a little frostily, "Some of us are."

After talking to Jan I'd rung Sarah. "No sweat! I owe you one, Tor."

More than one in fact, but who was counting? Sarah was a freelance who somehow never seemed to make any money but had contacts worth their weight in gold. She was also the only person I knew who'd be able to question the street kids who hung around Leicester Square. Blade had warned me against the direct approach but I didn't need warning. About three years ago, in a teenage runaway case, I'd swanned up to some lads festooned in tattoos and safety pins, flashed a photo at them and airily exhibited a five-pound note. One of them had gently flicked the fiver from between my fingers, shoved it down the front of his jeans and spat in my face. I'd gone back to the agency and rung Sarah; two hours later she'd rung back, case solved. This morning she'd promised to do what she could.

I looked down the list again and felt a twist of panic deep in my gut. What the fuck did I think I was up to? Arsing around like this, I was taking things about as seriously as Eleanor. And, I told myself bitterly, for the same reasons. I was so horny with the thought of April that I'd done nothing concrete to protect her at all. Don't get emotionally involved — well, it was too late for that.

From now on this had to be for real. I'd tell her I was a private detective and I'd approach this as I would any case, starting at the beginning, going through it with her step by step. The thought of telling her sent another stab of pain through my stomach. I didn't know how she'd react at all.

* * * * *

She didn't react particularly well to anything I had to say. "You heard me, Tor!" Her hair was scraped back in a brusque plait, the skin around her eyes tight. I could feel her exasperation from across the table. "There was no way I was going to keep it. I asked Antony to get it out of the house. He was going to College and he said he'd dump it in one of the industrial bins."

"April! I told you not to throw it away!"

"*Told?*" Her eyes were steel. "What *is* this? Why the fuck do you want to see a dead rat?"

"I'm not interested in the rat," I hissed. "I'm interested in what the package could have told us. How was it addressed? Was it handwritten? Where was it posted?"

"I don't give a flying fuck where it was posted! I'm not going to let something stupid like this screw everything up for me. Don't you understand? I'm juggling a hundred things at once, I can't afford to let this make me drop everything else. I need support from you, I don't need paranoia. And I definitely don't need you playing at amateur sleuth!"

I deserved the amateur bit, but it still stung. I opened my mouth to reply but she went on. "Look, I know you're worried and I know you've been asking questions and stuff. But let it drop."

So much for Jo's promises.

She smiled grimly. "Yesterday I had a chore to do the other side of town so I called in at the co-op. Ali said you'd been in there and she'd heard Jo say something about you playing detective. I didn't mention it last night because I didn't want us to argue."

"I don't want us to argue either, but you should know I'm not playing."

"All right, all right, I've got the message. I know you think this is all terribly serious."

"Too right, it's bloody serious. But what I meant is that I'm not playing at detective. I *am* a detective." I added hastily, "A private one."

She gave me the sort of look you give someone after they've just announced they're Cleopatra. Not Cleopatra reincarnated, Cleopatra in the flesh.

"You're what?"

"I'm a private detective, April. I'm sorry I didn't tell you before but I wasn't sure how you'd feel about it." I was astounded by the lameness of this. Why *hadn't* I told her?

April looked pretty astonished too; she let her cup clatter back onto its saucer then put her palms flat on the table and took a breath. "Is it me who's going off my head or just the rest of the world? You're telling me you're not an archivist?" She was blinking, hard.

I reached across the table and took both her hands. "I am, but I'm also a private detective, an investigator. That's what I was working as in New York. I've been doing it for years now, I got involved through my archival work, spotting forgeries, stuff like that. It's not a big deal."

Her fingers pulled out from under mine. "In other words you do divorce work," she said scathingly. "Following the wife around and spying on her for her old man. I guess it must be a bit like working for *News of the World*, counting the milk bottles on the doorstep and going through the rubbish bins."

Behind us the waiter coughed discreetly. "That's all, thanks," I said without looking up. And then straight at April, "I don't do divorce work. What I do is work on cases like yours, cases the police would laugh out of the station. I admit I haven't shone in this instance but then I've been working with a considerable handicap. First of all I was stupid and I didn't tell you when we met." Her mouth pursed but she didn't look away. "And, secondly, my mind hasn't been on the job. I'm in love with you. I haven't exactly been thinking straight."

April finished her coffee in a gulp. "I apologize about the *News of the World* crack but you have to admit this is all pretty surreal. Someone is trying to make me crazy by sending dead rats through the post. And then you announce you're Miss Marple."

"Yeah." I nodded. "I'm sorry for not telling you before. Do you forgive me? And do you mind if I ask you a few more questions?"

She didn't say whether she forgave me, but she did say she minded about the questions. Tomorrow, she said. Now she was going home, alone. I had no need to worry, she was quite safe, she wasn't going out anywhere tonight. She'd ring me at College in the morning and we could meet for lunch.

What could I say? "April ..." I was the one blinking now.

"I know." She sounded exhausted. "But I need to be by myself tonight."

Twenty minutes later the waiter came over and removed my cup. "Cheer up," he said, flashing me an understanding smile, "*I* don't believe you do divorce work."

116

CHAPTER THIRTEEN

Ma never approved of divorce, and if people were divorced she thought they shouldn't remarry. "Till death do us part," she'd say, her mouth a thin gash. She'd been in love with my father, how could she ever love anyone else? She'd told him she'd love him forever and she did.

When I told April I loved her it didn't mean the sort of love my mother had for my father, washing him in bed with warm flannels, turning him every two hours so he didn't develop bedsores, holding his head so he could manage a spoon. What I really meant when I said I loved April was that I would like to love her, I wanted to be given the chance to know her well enough to love her. You don't stay celibate for the rest of your life if someone you've slept with twice walks away at the end of the week. You don't kill yourself. Ma used to say if it hadn't been for me and Tim she would have killed herself when my father died, just swum out to sea and never stopped swimming. And I believe she would have.

Now it was possible I might never get the chance to know April well enough to love her in any of the numerous ways that mean love. She felt deceived. Worse, she saw me as part of the unexpected, bewildering flux that was currently her life. Rats in brown paper parcels, tattooed men, lovers who ... who what? What does a private detective *do*?

The first thing they do is disappear into the ladies powder room and splash their face with some cold water. They then cycle to College and check the industrial bins, just like a good tabloid hack. I poked my head over the edge, faced an impenetrable, soggy sea of food scraps in each, said shit a few times, then got back on my bike.

To top it all off my period had started. I took two painkillers and then forced myself to get back to the list. Tick off Bernard; a question mark still next to "Prince" ...

And then what, what does a detective do then? With nothing to go on, without even a client on the other side of the table?

I rang Sarah, who wasn't home.

Alicia wasn't home either.

Rosemary came in and I told her about the rat.

Eleanor walked in, listened in silence, then said it was obvious something had to be done, she'd ring the student counseling service tomorrow.

I walked out, knocking my chair over in the process. Halfway down the garden I heard raised voices.

"Victoria."

"C'est moi." I closed the notebook and made room for Rosemary on the sofa.

"Don't worry, Eleanor won't be contacting the psychologists."

"Glad to hear it."

"Term's as good as over so we might go away for a while, we could both do with a break. Eleanor has a cousin near Weymouth, we can go there."

"That's a good idea." I squeezed her hand and stroked a strand of hair back from her forehead. Her eyes were red and puffy. So much for love. "I love you, Rosemary," I said. Because that sort of love is important too.

The next morning I was at College by eight-thirty, firstly, so I tried to kid myself, because I had a lot of work to do, and secondly because I'd been awake since five, and thirdly because I was waiting for April's call. The waiting made it hard to concentrate on "An Adventure in the British Museum" and my transcription had more square brackets in it than usual. This morning I was finding whole sentences of John Llewelyn's normally reasonable hand almost indecipherable.

Rosemary walked in, dumped her briefcase on the

floor and looked over my shoulder. "Ow!" She shrugged off her jacket. "That looks painful."

"You mean my transcription? I'm sorry, I just can't get it right this morning, I'll come back later and fill in the gaps."

"I meant what the hero is getting up to with the Greco-Roman sculpture."

"Oh, that."

"She hasn't rung yet I take it."

The phone rang. As I lifted the receiver Rosemary waved and walked out.

It wasn't a good line. And the reason it wasn't a good line was that April was ringing from a call box at the station. "Jen called late last night," she was saying, "to tell me Gareth's got an ear infection. He can't sleep and he's been crying for me."

"And?"

"And I'm a mother for Christ's sake!"

Don't do this to me. I was in danger of developing a distinct whimper myself. My voice grated, "I appreciate that April, but you could have rung me last night, we could have met before the ten o'clock train. I thought we'd agreed it was necessary to talk?"

There was a brief silence. "We did, it is. But not now, Tor, I'm still too confused. Most of all I'm too tired. I feel like I've been run over by a truck."

That made two of us. "So when then? When are you coming back?"

"Monday maybe, or Tuesday . . ."

"April . . ." The whimper came out as a whine.

"But we can talk before then, I'll ring you Saturday night. Will and Jen are going out, so I'll be alone and we can talk. I'll think about everything over the next couple of days and I'll tell you if I can come up with any clues as to what this is all about." Her words sounded more encouraging than her tone. "Look, the train's due in about one minute so I've got to go. We'll talk Saturday." She hung up.

There was a subdued knock and Rosemary returned. "Stay there," she ordered, although I hadn't got as far as thinking about moving. She stretched across me, opened a drawer and took out a file. "I'll be in the library, my dear. Bye."

After she left I wiped away a few tears then rummaged through my shoulder bag for the notebook. I'd tried ringing Sarah again last night but hadn't got past her answering machine. I hadn't tried her yet this morning because I'd been too scared I'd miss April's call. Now I dialed again, College might as well pay for it. The number was engaged.

Flipping through the notebook I re-read my notes, added a few underlinings, then checked in the back for the co-op's number.

"Yeah?" Ali answered. I gritted my teeth and asked for Jo.

"Hello, Jo, it's Tor. Look, I have a question which might sound crazy, but I'd be grateful if you could answer it." Grateful to Jo, well why not? Nothing could make me feel shittier than I felt already.

"Depends. What do you want to know?"

"What April was doing in your part of town the day before yesterday, before she came to the co-op."

There was some chat about this, a lot of chat in fact. How come I couldn't ask April that? What exactly was I up to? My part of the chat involved yesterday's parcel, followed by April's exodus to London on the grounds that her son was sick.

"I can remember her saying she'd had something to do in that part of town," I summed up, "and I've been wondering if she was over there because of the sex shop."

"You've been wondering right," Jo admitted. "April went to the shop to deliver a letter from the anti-porn group, telling the management that from now on there'll always be at least three protesters posted outside. In fact ..." She hesitated, then went on, "This is a secret, but members of the group have been watching the shop every night for the past week. Only a handful of people know about it and I shouldn't be telling you anything."

"Can you tell me *why* they're watching the place?"

"It seems they don't just sell videos, we're pretty sure they're making them too. Women have been seen going in through the back door after opening hours and coming out much later."

I didn't know what to make of that, except that it sounded unlikely to me. The management had probably been entertaining on the premises, trying out the latest in bedroom appliances.

Jo laughed. "So you haven't been the only one doing the detective bit. Seems like there's a lot of it around these days."

"Seems like. Anyway thanks for the help."

"Anytime." She laughed again.

I hung up first.

Sarah's number was still engaged so on the spur of the moment I scribbled a note to Phoebe suggesting lunch, and took it along the hall to her pigeonhole. When I got back to Rosemary's room I redialed and this time got a reply.

"Prince is an interesting lad," Sarah mumbled; she was eating a honey and peanut butter sandwich.

"In what way?" It wasn't just the sandwich, this was a normal Sarah build-up. I knew from experience there was no point in trying to hurry her.

"Because he's not just into the gear and the aggro, he's into other stuff as well."

"What other stuff?"

There were more sandwich noises, followed by a faint burp. "Apparently he disappears from view every so often and it's rumored he does jobs, dirty jobs." She sounded pleased with herself. "And on the Friday in question he took off, telling one of his mates he was taking a train ride out into the country."

"Sounds like our man."

"That's what I thought. I put a photo of him in the post this morning, you can even see the tattoo."

She'd progressed from pleased to smug and I was in danger of being tearfully grateful. "Sarah thank you, this is a huge help." All I wanted to do was help, couldn't April see that?

"It was nothing," Sarah said. "I merely pretended to be an American tourist. I asked could I take his photo please, the folks back in Tallahassee would never believe it, and he said yes and then tried to menace some serious dosh out of me. Young Prince — given name, by the way, Derrick — is into making money whenever the opportunity arises, and according to my source you were quite right about the kinky sex."

"Businessmen who are into a bit of rough trade?"

"Rumor has it very rough, 'cause Selwyn gets a kick out of it that way. And not only businessmen, also business*women*."

"Do you believe that?"

"You'll have to take my informant's word for it, I'm not going to try him out for you. You know me, Tor, I like my men clean enough to eat off. I also prefer them not to be fascists. Call me fussy."

Next I rang April's house where the phone was answered by a quietly-spoken elderly woman with a local accent, presumably the scout, Mrs. Harvey. I asked if I could speak to Antony but she said he wasn't in, however she'd heard him tell one of the other students that he expected to be back around three.

"Right, then, I'll call round later. If he isn't back will there be someone I can leave a message with?"

"That's no problem dear, I'll be here myself till four."

The day was chilly, and halfway down St. Giles Phoebe and I ditched the idea of sandwiches in the University Parks.

"Which is it to be then?" Phoebe asked. "The Lamb and Flag or The Bird 'n Babe?"

I'd been to the former, but couldn't remember having seen the latter. "Where is it?" I asked.

"I keep forgetting you're not a local," she sighed and led the way into The Eagle and Child.

I bought us both a drink and asked for news on the Malcolm front. There were things I wanted to talk to her about other than her sex life but I needed to unwind a bit first.

Phoebe, meanwhile, was in excellent form. "Chest hair —" She ran her tongue along the edge of a Cornish pasty, "— like you wouldn't believe. A hard belly, with those cute little muscles. And the biggest —"

"Enough!" I actually meant it. "I want to be able to say hello to the guy without thinking about the size of his equipment, okay?"

"Okay." She took a bite and then returned the pasty to its plate. "So what's up, Tor? There's something on your mind. Am I right?"

"Yes Pheebes, you most certainly are."

I'm not entirely sure why I felt I needed to tell Phoebe about being a private detective, a desire for confession maybe. Fear that if I didn't she'd feel betrayed too, like April.

"So you weren't working in an archive in New York at all?"

"No, I'd done some work for this New York agency before, checking some letters that had been posted from London, and when I arrived in New York I contacted them."

"No kidding, it was that easy? It must be great being able to get a job in New York just like that."

Phoebe's eyes were very bright and I resigned myself to the next half hour. I'd been hoping we'd be able to talk about April's reaction to my choice of career, but it was pretty obvious that Phoebe was more interested in talking job opportunities.

* * * * *

At three o'clock Antony still wasn't back but Mrs. Harvey was at work in the kitchen. She'd watched April unwrap the parcel and was quite ready to talk about it. "A disgusting thing to do, April was so upset and I don't blame her. I felt off color myself for the rest of the day." And yes, she did know where it had been posted. "You'll think I'm a nosey old woman but I live alone and the students are all my family now so I take an interest. The parcel came from central London. The writing was in blue pencil, very untidy, and I remember thinking maybe it was a present from her son, something he'd made at school."

Not only that but she was sure it had been posted second class, on Saturday, which ruled out April's warning visit to the sex shop as the motivating factor.

Rosemary and Eleanor were hoping to get to Weymouth in time for dinner. I waved them off then spent the evening in front of the television, channel-hopping between *Mastermind* and *Cagney and Lacey* and trying hard not to think about anything too much. After a couple of liberal brandies I went to bed early, quickly falling into dreams that lurched into nightmare. The white-clad figure in the stern of the punt turned and growled with the face of a bulldog. "Eat this," it commanded, holding out a bouquet of dead flowers. I screamed and jumped overboard, while from somewhere behind a woman's voice shouted, "Off with her head!"

PART THREE

CHAPTER FOURTEEN

I did eventually fall out of bed, and as I walked in the back door I heard the phone ring in Rosemary's study.

Shock is a great soberer.

It took ten minutes to get dressed and cycle to April's house. I arrived in time to see a stretcher covered by a grey blanket. At the bottom of the steps a policewoman kept a small crowd of onlookers back while a reporter tried on a few questions.

"That's not hers ..." My voice came from a long way away.

"Sorry?" His pen hovered in mid air.

"That blanket, it isn't hers."

"Uh, I think the ambulance people provide them. Look, would you like to sit down, Miss?"

"No." Somewhere a girl was crying.

The pen hesitated again. "I'm right in thinking you're a resident aren't I? Can you tell me the victim's full name?"

As the stretcher came down the path I moved forward. Someone called for me to stop but I was there already, the pavement lurching beneath my feet as a corner of grey revealed a tangle of blonde hair streaked with blood. From behind, the policewoman's hand was urgent on my shoulder. "Oh hell," I heard her say, "she's going to faint."

As it turned out I *did* faint — not then but an hour or so later. For now, I turned round and stumbled back up the path toward home. I sat in the summerhouse and cried myself numb and then looked up to see through the window the figure of a young woman with long blonde hair. The figure came closer, held a lilac branch back from the window, smiled, and tapped loudly on the glass. *That* was when I fainted.

Luckily, I landed on the sofa bed.

"Tor, I'm here, you haven't been abandoned." There was a nervousness in her voice, as though she was very pleased I was so pleased to see her but also taken aback by the weeping, not to mention the fainting. "I had no idea that you were this upset." She sat me up, an arm around my shoulders. "Oh, Tor, did you think I'd really left you? That it was all over? This isn't the end, Tor, it's only the beginning." She hugged me hard but I pushed away from her.

"I didn't think you'd fucking left me, I thought you were *dead!*"

"Dead! What are you talking about, sweetheart? Why did you think I was dead?" The nervousness had turned into amusement and I looked up to see her eyeing the half-empty bottle of brandy.

I tugged at her arm and she turned back to me. "I'm not smashed, April! I thought you were dead because Deborah rang me and told me. And anyway —" I looked at her more closely. "I watched them carry your body out on a stretcher . . ."

On the train to London April had run into her Canadian friend, David. He was on his way to meet a cousin who'd just arrived from Berlin. There'd been a mixup over the guest room David had booked at his college and April had handed over her key and said of course his cousin Erich could have her room for the night. Erich was a mathematics student, on holiday in England for the first time. He was eighteen and had long blond hair, which was how David was going to be able to recognize him at Paddington.

April spent half an hour explaining to a detective-inspector, confirming what he'd already been told by David, who'd shown up at the house just after I, and the ambulance, had left. I then spent twice as long desperately attempting to convince the same detective-inspector that April's life was in danger and that whoever had been threatening her had killed Erich by mistake.

"A private investigator, you say?" Detective Inspector Thomson had winked at the policewoman. He eventually checked my credentials by ringing Alicia in London, but was still unconvinced by my arguments, even when I handed over the photo and description of Prince.

"All you have to do is find him," I said for the umpteenth time. "He's already threatened her once. He mightn't be the murderer, but if he's not, he'll know who's behind this."

"And you think someone put him up to threatening Miss Tate last Friday night and they knew when she'd be coming back to Oxford because she'd put a note in the student log book. Is that right?"

"I think it's a possible explanation, yes." I'd told him this twice already; he finally seemed to be catching on.

"But," he said, leaning forward and playing with his pen, "this week Miss Tate wrote in the book that she didn't expect to be back before next Tuesday, at the earliest. So anyone checking the book last night wouldn't expect to find her in her room, would they?" He gave a victorious grin. "How do you explain that?"

His explanation was that the threatening letters weren't to be taken seriously. They could be a matter of student rivalry, or — here he lined the pen straight along the edge of the table — jealousy.

A jilted boyfriend? No? As for the skinhead, town and gown tension in Oxford went back to the twelfth century. The students and the local teenagers were always having run-ins. Last night was a terrible tragedy, the burglars probably thought most students had already left for the vacation. They obviously didn't expect to find anyone at home and had panicked when Erich challenged them. A number of similar break-ins had taken place recently and the police were already following up several good leads.

As April and I walked in Rosemary and Eleanor's front door the phone rang and the policewoman I'd seen at the station informed me that Detective Inspector Thomson had checked out the whereabouts of "Prince," aka Derrick Jones, and as a result he had been eliminated from the inquiry.

"Oh, thanks." I counted to three and managed to keep my tone even. "Can you tell me why?"

She hesitated for a moment then lowered her voice. "Well, I shouldn't really say any more but it seems that Mr. Jones was in police custody in central London last night, on a drunk and disorderly." She couldn't hide the smugness as she added, "So he can't also have been in Oxford can he?" The rest of the message was that her boss thanked me for my help and hoped this information would put my mind at rest.

Everything was going horribly wrong so it didn't really surprise me that April agreed with the police about it being a burglary. "Because I'd know if someone hated me *that* much." She stretched out on the living room's blue carpet, a cushion under her head.

"I see. Then how come you don't know who it is that's been sending you dead rats?"

"Hate mail's one thing, murder's something else. There's no connection here, Tor, believe me." Ever since she'd realized that I'd really thought she was dead, April had been handling me with kid gloves. Which was just how I needed to be handled.

"Tor?"

"Mmmm." I was mentally compiling a new list.

"I'm going to get us something to eat and then I'd better go and see Deborah. When I spoke to Mrs. Harvey she said Debs was okay, but I'd like to talk to her myself. Maybe you should stay here and take a nap ..."

"There's no need for that. I'll come too." I had news for April Tate, she wasn't going anywhere by herself until I knew who'd tried to kill her.

After visiting Deborah I spent an hour on the phone, and when it came time for bed we slept in the house.

"Why?" April was disappointed. "The summerhouse is much more fun. Besides, think of the extra work, more sheets to wash ..."

"There's a machine," I said grimly. "Anyway, I think you should move in here permanently. I'm sure Rosemary and Eleanor wouldn't mind."

"Stop it, Tor, I'm not in danger. If you're that worried about me you'll just have to sleep with me every night, won't you?"

She grinned but I didn't grin back, I was too busy making sure all the windows were shut securely.

CHAPTER FIFTEEN

Over the weekend I found myself thinking that the fates were kind. But where then did that leave the boy with the long blond hair? What did he do to die at eighteen? In my story he doesn't even get a walk-on part, while for someone else he's a lifetime's tragedy. You wake up and find someone searching the room, my professional advice is to act like you're still asleep. That way you're less likely to get hit over the head with a blunt instrument or, as in this case, stabbed in the throat with an eight-inch blade.

We had a number of visitors. Deborah, Jo and Blade. And David — who was flying to Germany to see Erich's parents on Monday. I rewrote my list a few times and asked April as many questions as she was willing to put up with. April filled vases with greenery in the mornings and in the afternoons I traced red wine across her breasts ... In bed at night I sat up reading.

"What are you doing?" Half asleep, she nuzzled her head against my side.

"Reading. I'm okay. Go back to sleep."

"Watching out for bears ..."

"What was that?"

"Bears, Tor." She climbed back onto the pillow. "You're keeping the bears away."

Well, I was trying.

Sarah got back to me early on Monday evening. I took the call in Rosemary's study.

"Gone? You mean he's gone away for a few days or he's left for good?" I demanded.

"He cleared all his stuff out from the squat he was living in and left a couple of boxes of records and tapes with his mother. She thinks he hocked his ghetto blaster to pay for his ticket."

"His mother?"

"Come on, Tor, even skinheads have mothers. He turns up on her doorstep whenever he's really in trouble — considering everything, he's not in trouble all that often. Looks after himself fairly well does young Prince."

"You've talked to her then? And what do you mean ticket? Ticket where?"

"One thing at a time! Yes, I have talked to her. She doesn't know where he was going, but he said he was leaving the country for a while — he's done it a couple of times before, cleared off to Amsterdam once for over six months. She doesn't know if that's where he's headed this time, all he'd say was that he was fed up and needed to get away for a while."

"Did he mention the drunk and disorderly charge?"

"No, but I don't think he'd bother about something that minor. I don't think that counts as serious."

"I don't suppose there's any way of finding out if he is in Amsterdam?"

"He's not in Amsterdam, he's in France, probably Paris. Or at least he was — he might have left already, of course."

"You're amazing! How did you trace him?"

Sarah didn't try too hard to sound modest. "No sweat. There was a new Metro map in with the cassettes and I just happen to have a very good friend who works for immigration ..."

I butted in straight away, "This is for money now, you know. Just send me your bill."

"No financial transactions involved. Don't worry, if there had been I'd certainly tell you."

Sarah no longer owed me, I owed her. Which is how these things work.

She went on, "He caught a ferry to Cherbourg, but, as I said, who knows for certain where he's gone from there? I've contacted someone who'll keep an eye out, but it's a long shot. In Amsterdam he might be traced fairly easily but in Paris it's easier to disappear, even if you are an English-speaking skin."

"Thank you anyway, you've been a huge help." My mind was racing ahead but Sarah still deserved some back-patting. "How did you get his Mum to show you what was in the boxes?"

"Said I was a youth worker ... But hold on, Tor, there's more to come. We had a cuppa and discussed young Prince at some length. The most interesting thing she told me was that he'd been expelled from school ..."

"You do surprise me."

"He was expelled from school ..." She was taking it so slow she could have spelled it out, "after he killed a white rat in front of one of the teachers. He put it on her desk and smashed its head in with a hammer."

Alicia rang a few hours later, her voice weary.

"You sound exhausted."

"Completely knackered. The case I've been on for two weeks blew badly yesterday, I don't even want to think about it. What about you? How are the police performing?"

"All we've heard is that we'll have access to April's room from ten tomorrow morning. I'll go over it of course but they've had more than enough time to trample everything."

"And April still can't come up with any clues?"

"Nothing. We had a session this morning, and again this afternoon. We didn't come up with a thing, not even something like a life insurance policy. She's got a few ex-lovers, yes, but none sound at all crazy, and Ellen, who she amicably broke up with eight months ago, is currently living very happily in Tanzania with a seriously rich widow."

"Well someone out there isn't very happy about something."

"Tell me about it. I know you've been busy but have you had time to look into anything for me?"

"I have, and the answer's no."

"Shit."

"Come on, Tor, you didn't really expect anything did you?"

"Well, you never know: rabid, born-again in-laws who resent the fact that their son's wife is a dyke. In order to protect their beloved grandchild from Satan they pay a hit-man to murder her. I could run with that."

"You and _The Sun_ maybe. You're right about the religious bit though. Plus, of course, they've both got criminal records."

"What?" I was briefly hopeful.

"Yep, a dangerous lot, these Quakers, they got done some years ago for taking wire cutters to the Greenham fence. Sorry, but no go, Tor. Anyway, what about April's own parents? Maybe they don't approve of their daughter's new life."

"But they do," I replied miserably, my list of

suspects shrinking all the time. "They encouraged her to come out, being good liberals and all that."

"So what now?"

"I don't know, Alicia, I really don't know."

First thing Tuesday morning Bernard was all efficiency and not a little peeved that Rosemary and Eleanor weren't at their posts. "A murder takes place and the Dean's gone on holiday!" he boomed over the phone.

Rosemary hadn't given me a number for Weymouth but she had rung the previous night, just after Alicia, and I'd given her the news. She'd said they'd leave for Oxford at the crack of dawn.

"They expect to be back by nine at the latest," I told him.

"Hasn't she been reading the papers? I could have done with Dr. Litton's presence two days ago. There have been the police to deal with, and the press. Luckily Detective Inspector Thomson appreciates that I have College to run. His men have finished at the house and the Bursar tells me the scout's cleaning the room this morning and the French doors have been repaired. New furniture will also be put in."

So much for my having a look around.

"You can tell Mrs. Tate," he spat out, "that the maintenance staff will help her move rooms at midday. You can also tell her I expect her in my office at two. I hold her personally responsible for this tragedy."

"You *what*?" It was my turn to spit.

"As she well knows, it is against College rules to give an outsider keys to any of the houses without the Bursar's permission. She had no right allowing that young man to stay in her room, and if she'd followed the rules he'd be alive now. In fact I think she deserves to be sent down."

I told Bernard I had no intention of passing on the last half of his message. I also told him that if he tried to put any blame on April I'd have a word with a journalist friend who, I was willing to bet, would jump at a story about sexual harassment in a certain Oxford institution ...

"I'll carry your plants for you, April." Deborah was still wearing a dazed look. April was busy putting books into a cardboard box and didn't hear.

"Thanks, Deb, that's great," I replied.

The furniture changes had involved the removal of the blood-stained green carpet and the bed. The new bed wasn't new at all and the mattress looked decidedly uncomfortable.

Antony frowned at it, then shrugged. "You'll find the one upstairs just as bad, I'm afraid. As for this brown carpet ... Still, I can stagger in here late at night and not disturb anybody, and I can play my music at all hours."

"Thank you, Antony," said April as she passed the box of books to one of the maintenance men. "Offering to swap was heroic, I didn't really fancy moving back in."

"My motives are purely selfish, I assure you. I'd better go back upstairs and unplug the stereo since we have staff here to help fetch and carry. It's amazing you know, even if you're moving across Oxford, College never does more than offer you an enormous great trolley that it takes two people to get moving — even when there's nothing on it. This is a new experience, I can tell you."

I shoved a couple of cushions at him to carry. "This is all because of the old boys' network. Usually the police would still have this room taped shut, but your Principal's obviously had a word with someone high up. An Oxford routine can't be disrupted."

Antony balanced a ring binder of April's law notes on the cushions. "How do you know things like that?"

"Like what? Like Oxford principals having friends in high places? That's how they get to be principals in the first place."

"No, like how long the police would normally keep the room shut up. I didn't even know they used tape and stuff until I saw them putting it on the doors."

Picking up a pile of clothes on hangers and leading the way to the door, I said, "That just shows what a sheltered life you've led, Antony."

April started organizing her bookshelves. I cycled into town and visited a hardware shop where I had myself some keys cut to the house and her room, and also bought some sturdy bolts for the windows and door. As I'd said to my great aunt a few weeks earlier, bolts aren't ideal, but they're better than nothing. I spent the rest of the afternoon fiddling with a screwdriver. Mrs. Harvey popped her head round the door every so often but although she nodded in approval she didn't comment.

While I faffed about security, Antony seemed to have nothing on his mind beyond interior decorating and was even discussing taking up the carpet and painting the floorboards. "Wouldn't the Bursar have something to say about that?" I asked.

"Normally quite a lot I should think. But, let's face it, all I have to say is that I've discovered bloodstains in a corner, that will shut them up PDQ. I mean, number thirteen and a murder to boot! The Bursar positively drooled her gratitude when I told her I was moving in." He eyed my handiwork. "Why the bolts? Surely the first floor is fairly burglar-proof?"

"Just between the two of us I'm not sold on the burglar theory."

"Are you thinking about that horrid business with the rat?"

"Yes, and it seems silly to take risks."

"I can see your point although I really don't think you should get paranoid. That Detective Inspector what's-his-face . . ."

"Thomson."

"Well, he said there have been a number of burglaries in this area recently. You can see how it could happen, a couple of small-time crooks break in, then panic."

"Possible," I said. "By the way, have you checked the repairs to the French doors? I would, if I were you."

He shrugged. "Oh all right, if it will stop you worrying."

144

* * * * *

Rosemary, looking shattered, called by in the afternoon. I took her for a stroll round the garden.

"The police are sure it's a botched burglary ..." She hesitated briefly. "But I assume you're worried in case it's not that simple."

"Worried is an understatement. Look, I'll be staying here most of the time now, I'm not going to leave her alone. If the Bursar finds out and causes trouble can I ask you to protest on my behalf?"

"Of course."

"And I'll be able to finish the transcriptions but the hours I do might be a bit erratic. Do you mind?"

If she did I'd hand in my notice. But I didn't expect any hassle from Rosemary, and I didn't get any. "You know I don't mind. Making sure that April is safe is the most important thing. I must say she seems to be coping extraordinarily well."

"That's because she agrees with the police."

"I thought she might."

"She's not going to like it but I'm going to do my best to make sure there's always someone around. I just hope she doesn't decide I'm the complete nutter."

"Maybe a word from me would help?"

"You want to tell her there's never been any madness in the family? It's not true, you know."

"I was thinking more along the lines of your having had a rather heavy time of it. First of all the death of your mother, then Alicia and New York ... I could gently suggest that this has stirred lots of things up and it might be an idea if we all humor you for a while."

145

"You're brilliant."

Rosemary went back into the house to have her chat with April and I sat on the garden seat and wondered why she hadn't said anything about Eleanor.

That evening we christened the new room with a Chinese meal. I poured jasmine tea for both of us and did some smooth talking. "... it won't be a problem," I smiled reassuringly, "and it will make me feel a whole lot happier."

"All right." April put her head on one side. "I don't mind telling you my timetable and having an escort for a while." Rosemary had done her job like an expert, April kept shooting me understanding looks.

"Just for a few weeks."

"Weeks!" She didn't sound understanding now, just stunned. "Tor, I thought you meant a few days. A week at the most."

I blinked rapidly. We compromised at ten days.

"Okay?" She passed me a battered prawn.

"I guess it'll have to be."

After April assured me that she wasn't planning on leaving the house, and would be quite safe watching television with Deborah, I caught a taxi to Jo and Blade's flat.

"You're a private *eye*?" Jo hit her forehead in mock angst. "And to think I presented you with a complimentary copy of *Gaudy Night!*"

I didn't bother to correct her. Blade gave Jo an odd look then turned thoughtfully to me. "I'll help

146

you," she said and out of the corner of my eye I could see her lover's look of surprise. "Jo works, but all I have to do is sign on. I'll do whatever I can."

I could have kissed her, but not in front of Jo. Instead we solemnly shook hands.

CHAPTER SIXTEEN

April slipped some bread under the grill and glanced across at Blade, who was staring moodily into her mug of coffee. "Don't mind me," she'd said when she'd arrived ten minutes earlier, "I'm not worth a dead fag end at this time of the morning."

April looked back at me, "Your detective work" she said, "it's a way of empowering women isn't it?"

It was a nice idea but the heady idealism made me a touch nervous. "Not all my clients are women."

"All right, it's a way of empowering people who can't get any joy out of the system."

People who could afford to pay, I thought to myself. This morning the sky was blue and April was wearing a calf-length red skirt and red sweatshirt. Her hair was tied up in a green scarf. I was wearing black. Last night I'd come back via Rosemary and Eleanor's in order to collect a few more clothes. Everything I'd hauled out of the wardrobe and drawers was black. Some coincidence: the tension that had formerly played April had transferred itself to me. As she leaned back against the refrigerator and convinced herself of the ideological correctness of private detection I could feel a familiar, tell-tale tic beginning under my right eye. I thought the tic and I had parted company on the plane out of JFK airport. I'd thought wrong.

"When did you start rethinking your attitude toward privatized crime prevention?" I asked. Despite everything I hadn't forgotten her divorce quip.

"On the train to London. Gareth's earache was a false alarm and by the afternoon I was missing you terribly."

As I'd said to Alicia, no known enemies or lunatic ex-lovers. Which left me with the sex shop. Blade escorted April to the law library and I cycled across town to the co-op.

"Thought you were supposed to be guarding April?" Jo was comparing two pieces of red card against the light. To me they looked identical but she seemed to think otherwise.

"Blade's with her. I wanted to talk to you."

She dumped one of the pieces of card in the bin.

"Give me ten minutes, till Ali gets back from her break. You can wait out in the garden if you like."

This time there was no blanket but the grass was warm against my back. A desultory vine trailed across one half of the brick wall at the end of the garden and across on the other half I began to imprint a mental list, the only problem being I had virtually nothing to put on it. 1) Talk to Jo about the sex shop. 2) Ring Sarah again to see if her Paris contact had come up with any news. 3) Wait for Alicia to get back to me. 4) Visit the sex shop tonight. This last point warranted a question mark. After that I hit blank wall, then vine. Right at the top a sparrow disappeared, worm in beak, which suggested a nest. A good omen surely?

"Ah, the cruelty of April." Jo must have followed my gaze.

"What?"

"Isn't April the cruel month, according to the poets? A mixture of lilacs, desire and memory if I remember my Eliot correctly."

I was glad I'd felt the need to paint on a face this morning. I grimaced with my blood-red mouth and looked down along the line of my black T-shirt, black trousers, black shoes. Red nails would be nice sometime. I hadn't painted mine in years. I dug my naked nails into my palms and sat up. There was too much at stake for any crap. Besides, Eliot's not my favorite poet.

"The sex shop, Jo."

"What about it?" She flopped down heavily beside me.

"I've been thinking about what you said about the possibility of porn videos being made there. If that's true then it's also possible somebody feels there's a lot at stake and any opposition has to be got out of the way."

This wasn't a long shot — it was a trip to Mars. Jo's face, however, lost the superior look it had taken on with the poetry and instead appeared interested. "Hey, you could be onto something there! I bet that's it!"

As she envisaged a dark porn empire with Oxford as its capital I listened and rested my eyes on the blankness of the wall. Yeah, I nodded, great. Privately I decided to invite Blade along tonight.

Twenty minutes later I unchained my bike and cycled back towards the town center. I'd only got a few yards when I noticed the white car ahead. It pulled to a stop and I slammed on the brakes alongside the driver's door.

"Christ." The woman in the seat swivelled round and looked up at me. "You gave me a fright, I thought I'd hit you!"

Her friend who was emerging from the passenger door was also startled. She shaded her eyes and peered at me across the car roof. "Have you come to join the picket?" On the pavement behind her three women and a man were holding up anti-pornography placards.

"Oh, sorry." I smiled weakly. "I thought you were someone else. Good luck!" and I cycled off cursing myself. What would that have achieved? I hadn't even thought about taking the number plate. What had I intended to do? Haul the driver out and give whoever it was a good thrashing? Trying to combine a murder case with True Love was proving a serious problem.

* * * * *

Later that night I had a few extra things to worry about, including a pile of fermenting garbage. "This is becoming a bit ridiculous," I muttered to Blade.

"No it's not, it's like Cagney and Lacey."

"That's sacrilege, you'd never find either of them stinking of stale kippers. Whose idea was this anyway?"

Blade shook her head. "I don't know who thought of it first, but the women from the anti-porn group have been hiding here every night."

From what Jo had told me they hid there behind the garbage, took photos of the manager and his companion going in, then waited to see how long they spent inside before coming out. I couldn't really see the point of the exercise but hadn't mentioned that to Jo in case it wasn't considered constructive.

The garbage bags were piled in a corner of the yard next to a couple of metal bins and about ten yards from the shop's back door. There was a large room on the ground floor at the back and this is where the photo sessions were suspected to be taking place. There were two high windows to the right of the steps that led up to the door, and on the ground between the windows were cardboard boxes and an old-fashioned tea chest — the sort you can never get hold of when you're moving house. I judged the distance from the windows to the tea chest then stood up.

Blade tugged at my sleeve in alarm. "They'll be here soon!"

"In five minutes precisely, if they keep to

schedule. Stay where you are Blade, I'll be back shortly."

I sauntered across the well-lit yard, conscious that an upstairs neighbor could be watching from over the wall. I decided there was only one window I could be seen from, and that one had its curtains pulled. I listened in case a car was coming down the side, then pulled the tea chest a couple of feet until it was under the window furthest from the steps. The chest wasn't that sturdy, but no doubt would take my weight if I positioned my feet at the edges. I then sprinted back to Blade and squatted back behind the black bags.

"Be careful you don't get spotted," Blade whispered. "Or he'll stop using this place before the group's got any real evidence."

"And what sort of evidence do they expect to get if they stay hidden down here?" I countered.

"Search me," she said. "I think you've got the right idea but we better not blow it ..."

As a car came down the drive she shut up and handed me the opera glasses which she'd already explained had belonged to Jo's grandmother. I settled down onto my haunches and positioned the glasses into the gap we'd made between two of the bags. Jo had said that each night the manager had shown up with a woman in her early thirties. Tonight, however, he hadn't come with any thirty-year-old: the girl hunched in the front seat looked fifteen at the most. And not only was she underage, she'd also been crying. I felt faintly sick; this wasn't what I'd anticipated at all.

He stopped the car, got out and went round to the back. The girl stayed where she was. When he saw she hadn't made a move he thumped on the roof with his fist. "Get out right now!" He retrieved a briefcase, slammed the trunk closed, then stormed round to the passenger side. "Marion, I'll not tell you again, now get out!"

Marion was about five-foot-five, wearing tight blue jeans and a pink shirt. Her dark hair was pulled back into a pony tail and despite her red-rimmed eyes I could see she was very pretty. Her companion thrust the briefcase at her then led the way, searching his pockets for his keys as he went. He opened the door and pushed the girl inside and a few seconds later the lights went on.

"We've got to do something!" Blade hissed at me.

"First of all we have to find out exactly what's going on." There was a sour taste at the back of my throat. "I'll give them fifteen minutes then I'll take my camera and climb up on the box. With luck I'll be able to see in."

"And if you can't?"

"We'll work something out. You can draw his attention to the front of the shop and I'll see if I can get in the back door — there must be a storeroom or something I could hide in."

"You mightn't like listening very much," Blade said bitterly. I suspected she was dead right. My legs had gone into cramp and I staggered erect.

"You're sure you'll be all right?" she asked. I nodded and walked across the concrete on the balls of my feet, trying to be quiet, and at the same time to get the blood flowing. At the tea chest I stopped and listened. There was a scraping sound from inside and then a male voice, very close and very angry.

"For Christ's sake! Aren't you ready yet?"

"I'm almost ready. I have to have something to drink first." Her voice was adolescent whiney.

"That's what you always say, you're just playing for time. I'll be back in one minute and I want you ready to start."

"But I don't want to do it!"

"You'll do as you're bloody told!" Footsteps headed in the direction of the front of the shop. There was the scraping noise again, as if something was being dragged across the floor, and then a radio clicked on.

I leaned forward and took hold of the far side of the box and then quickly lifted myself up onto one, and then two, feet. The box held and I slowly pulled myself up against the wall, resting my cheek against the edge of the wooden window frame. From inside John Peel was talking reassuringly about world music and over the top of his voice there came a ripping sound, as if material was being torn. I rolled my cheek across flaking paintwork and moved my right eye into position: all I could see was a sink with some coffee mugs sitting on the draining rack. There was an open door next to the sink but my view of the rest of the room was blocked by the back of a cupboard. There were footsteps and I rolled my face back.

This time the voice was more cheerful. "Being reasonable again, are we?"

"Funny idea you've got of what's reasonable."

"That's enough of that. For Christ's sake, Marion, how many times do I have to tell you that's not the way to hold the knife? Do you want to finish up in casualty?"

I flattened myself against the wall. Breathing in

one, two, three, holding — exhaling one, two, three. I then pushed outwards and sank down in one movement, the box wobbling ever so slightly.

As I got off and stood up there was a hand across my mouth. Fucking hell, where was Blade? The hand turned my face and there she was, a finger to her lips. She raised her eyebrows. I shook my head and pointed to the other window. Nodding she silently stepped sideways until she was to the left of the window, then beckoned.

As I drew next to her she squatted and pointed to her shoulders. She was slightly shorter than I, but more solidly built. I hesitated for a moment, thought of the girl inside, and straddled her shoulders. She stood straight up without a sound.

My face was to the left of the window and I edged it forward then rolled my left cheek sideways again. This time I could see straight in, to where Marion was sitting on a metal chair, her legs spread on either side of a cardboard box. She was still in her shirt and jeans but in her left hand she was holding the dildo I had seen in the shop, the one with the bowler hat and smiley face. Mr. Smiley. In her right she held what looked like a small gun.

"It's not really that bad, eh?" He reached out and patted her knee. Marion sniffed then appeared to shoot Mr. Smiley in the head. She was putting on prices.

"You know I wanted to go out tonight." She was reconciled now, and sounding more grown-up. "It's boring opening all these boxes."

"Mum's got flu, pet, and these have to be done." His voice was suddenly anxious. "You know we've told you there's nothing to be ashamed about, this is

just a business. We're doing a public service really."
He almost sounded as if he believed it.

"But it's silly, Dad!" Marion's hair was flung back
in distaste. "It's really silly, all this. And ..." She
hesitated then blurted out the awful truth. "Not only
is it silly, it's sexist!"

CHAPTER SEVENTEEN

I'd been awake half the night and couldn't bear lying rigid any longer. How did College do it? April's new bed was even narrower than the last had been. Doing my best not to wake her I slid out from under the duvet. I held the curtain slightly open to check the weather and there was Deborah, walking dreamily along the path to where the copper beech shone scarlet. It would be chilly outside. I pulled on the clothes I'd been wearing last night and went down to join her.

As I appeared in the kitchen doorway Deborah called softly that there was coffee in the percolator if I wanted some. I did. A couple of minutes later I was sitting next to her on the garden bench, warming my hands round a full mug. "Come here often, do you?" I teased.

She smiled. "This is my favorite time of day. I even saw a fox once."

"True?" I was surprised. "I didn't know there were foxes in Oxford's suburbia."

Deborah then told me about the fox she'd seen, its eyes green in the early light, the contents of a garbage bin scattered around its feet. Then, with some gentle prodding, she also told me how she'd felt the morning she'd found Erich's body. She'd seen April's French doors half open and had assumed that meant April was awake ...

"I knocked to ask if she wanted coffee. There was no answer, and then I noticed the blood on the door."

Blood was something Deborah knew about because at the age of eight she'd been trapped in the back seat of her parents' car after a truck had run into it. It had taken the police twenty minutes to get Deborah out and during that time her mother had bled to death. Her father had died as soon as the truck hit them.

"When I looked inside and saw all the blood over the bed and the carpet I knew April had to be dead — except it turned out that it wasn't April ..."

"No," my voice came as a distant echo. "It wasn't April."

Deborah hadn't screamed, she'd carefully turned

around and gone back into the kitchen, where she'd met Mrs. Harvey who'd just arrived for work. Mrs. Harvey hadn't panicked either but had walked down the hall to April's room. A couple of minutes later she came back and told Deborah that she was to go down the road to another student house where Deborah's friend Jane lived. She was to go there, Mrs. Harvey said, and Jane was to look after her.

Soon after Deborah arrived at Jane's place the street filled up with police cars, and then an ambulance. Deborah didn't go back to the house however — she'd seen enough. She watched Jane shakily pour whiskey into the cup of coffee she was clutching, and then pour a generous tumbler for herself. After they'd drunk that, Deborah realized there was something she could still do for April, and that was to tell her friend, Tor. Jane rang directory enquiries and asked for Dr. Rosemary Myers's number.

They hadn't known, of course, that I was staying in the summerhouse where there was no phone, nor that Rosemary and Eleanor were away. The phone rang and rang until I eventually answered. Later the police came to talk to Deborah and it was only then that she found out it wasn't April after all.

"I'm sorry to have scared you like that." Her voice was jagged and I reached out and squeezed her hand. "This had made me think about a lot of things," she went on, "about my parents dying, stuff like that. I feel now would be a good time to make a new start. I know this might seem silly but I'm going to have my hair cut!"

"Seems completely reasonable to me." Deborah's

hair was long and heavy and added to her air of vulnerability. "How short are we talking?"

She sounded more cheerful. "Oh I'm not going overboard. I used to know someone who's got thick hair like mine and I really like the way she wore it. Do you mind having a look at a photo, to see if you think it will suit me? I'll meet you back in the kitchen."

She headed into the house and I sat and finished my coffee and wondered what it was I was missing. I was missing something, I knew that much. There was a sense of something unseen, overlooked. It made me frightened, and angry, at the same time.

The dress on the young woman in the photo was navy blue and expensive, her skin was clear, her hair well-cut and glossy. Where Deborah's face was wide and open, the features in the photo were chiseled and would have been sharp but for the softness of the grey eyes. She was very attractive in a conventional way; Deborah wasn't so conventional-looking and as a result the haircut would look less fashionable. I also thought it would look better.

"Really, Deborah, it's a good choice."

"Do you think so?" She glowed and for a moment her happiness was infectious.

"I most certainly do. Who is she, anyway? Is she at College?"

"Her name's Susannah and her brother, Damian, used to live in the house. He didn't come back at the beginning of term and April moved into his room."

"Right. He got into some sort of trouble, didn't he?"

She nodded. "People say his father was angry with him. I know he took Damian to America to work in his company there. When Damian was here Susannah used to come and visit him. She was nicer than her brother, really."

"Do you still see her?" Deborah had a small but solid group of friends and you could tell she'd be the one who'd keep them in touch with each other.

"No, I didn't know her that well although I would have liked to get to know her better. She was here quite a lot last year because she went out with Antony for a while. But then they broke up and she didn't come back till the weekend when she and her mother packed up Damian's room. Her mother's nice too — they were really upset. This is Damian." She handed over a picture of the brother and sister sitting under the copper beech. "And this," she said with an apologetic little shrug, "is a photo of my parents."

Deborah's mother looked like an older Deborah, she had the same broad cheekbones, the same pink in the cheeks. She also had a fashionable haircut fairly similar to Susannah's.

Deborah and I had toast and then I took some fresh coffee up to April, who grumbled at being woken up.

"I thought you had work to do?"

"Sure do, but nothing that can't be done this afternoon." She yawned and sat up to take the mug.

"You look like a mermaid."

"Scales and a tail?"

"Your hair spread out like that, you look as if you should be sunning yourself on a rock, comb in hand." I'd kill anyone who tried to hurt her.

She smiled. "Not an impossibility you know, there is such a thing as the summer vacation. Will and Jen are going to Italy for two weeks and I'll run the bookshop while they're away, which will give me some money. So a couple of weeks on a Greek beach is quite feasible."

I wanted to go now, I wanted to be as far away from Oxford as I could get. The fairy castle had become sinister and gothic and I couldn't find my way out.

"Tor?"

"Yeah?" Oh shit, I was crying. April pulled me close and stroked my hair and told me over and over it was all all right.

We spent the rest of the morning in bed and when I climbed back into my clothes for the second time things didn't seem quite so bleak.

Blade arrived and I went off to have lunch with Rosemary and to check the answering machine for messages from Alicia or Sarah. I'd hauled the machine out of a cupboard after it had become clear I'd be living with April, and I wondered how Rosemary and Eleanor were coping with this intrusion of technology. The machine had been given to them two years ago and they'd learned to hate it by the end of the first week. I couldn't live without one, but could appreciate that not everyone's life revolves around the phone as much as mine.

Alicia's was the only message. I played back the tape and she said she had no news at her end and hoped I was okay. There was nothing from Sarah.

"Anything of interest?" Eleanor asked. I hadn't discussed any of my inquiries with her and wasn't sure how much Rosemary had passed on. Since I'd moved in with April, Eleanor had kept her distance, which hurt, but I was aware that she was hurting too. The inquiry about the answering machine was a heartening sign and I only wished I had something useful to report. I told her Alicia had rung but she hadn't come up with anything, and Eleanor patted my hand and said she was sure everything would be all right and I wasn't to be too concerned. She then went upstairs to do some work and I helped Rosemary clear the table.

I said, "Eleanor's still insisting that there's nothing to worry about, isn't she?"

Rosemary looked slightly embarrassed as she nodded.

"I take it she's still sold on the burglary theory?"

She nodded again then changed the topic. "I realize you've probably got too much on your plate at the moment but if you wanted to come, I'm doing a spot of work in the British Library tomorrow and could do with some help. All expenses paid of course. If the two of us go there'll be a morning's work between us. I have to be back here in the afternoon for a meeting but you could spend the day in London if you like."

I gave it about ten seconds thought. Blade could stay with April, so she wouldn't be alone. "Great," I said. A trip to London might prove quite useful.

After lunch I wandered down to the

summerhouse and decided on a going-to-London outfit: the black Chinese jacket and a smartly-cut red linen dress I'd bought at a seconds shop years ago. I'd never discovered what the flaw was supposed to be. I pulled a pair of new tights out of my suitcase and at the same time noticed an envelope of old photos. Why not? This evening I'd show April some of my family pictures.

We hadn't done much talking since the weekend and that had been okay. Now, though, I found there were things I wanted to talk about. Gareth for instance — I wanted to hear more about him. And about her parents too. At one stage I clambered off the bed to pour some wine and collected my photos on the way back. There was me aged four with Tim, Ma in a straw hat. And the father I'd never met, as a boy and then as a young man.

She sipped her wine and sat cross-legged. "You look more like him than your mother. He died before you were born?"

"Six weeks before, to the day."

"He looks nice. He's got your brown eyes, and your height.

"Come on now, I'm five-seven, he was six-two."

"You know what I mean. And you're both slim."

She shuffled through the photos and then came across the last one. After studying it for a few moments she looked up. "Is this what I think it is?"

"What do you think it is?" I felt slightly uncomfortable.

"I think I see your father in military uniform."

"Uh huh." I toasted both her and the photo.

"And on his uniform there's a medal ..."

"So there is."

"It's a VC, isn't it?"

"I believe so."

She drew her hair back from her face, as if she needed space to think. "He died, and your mother named you after the medal he'd won. That must have been terrible for her," she went on, "him dying before you were born. But it was nice her being able to name you Victoria. She must have been very proud of both of you. Why don't you use your full name anyway? I like it."

"I don't know, it just seems a bit of a mouthful."

"Victoria." April stretched her arms wide. "Victoria Cross, come here."

CHAPTER EIGHTEEN

Rosemary and I finished in the library early. She took the opportunity to get back to Oxford well before her meeting and I took myself off to Covent Garden where I bought an orange juice at one of the outdoor cafes and watched a trio of jugglers performing with eggs, wine glasses, flaming torches ...

"... she must have been very proud of you." Well yes, at first I'm sure she had been, though as a child I found being named after my dead father's war medal something of an unwelcome responsibility.

167

And then, at the end ... I suspected that at the end Ma deeply regretted having named me as she did.

The waitress glared at my empty glass but I figured that the amount I'd paid for the juice could count as half an hour's rent. I spent another quarter of an hour watching a fire-eater, and then set off for the agency.

The young black woman at the desk would be Andrea, Janet's replacement. We hadn't met, but just as I'd heard about her, she'd obviously heard about me.

"Ms. Cross?"

Ms. Cross? Ms. Formal. All the same, I nodded.

"Alicia is talking to a client. She should be finished soon. Would you like to take a seat?"

I glared across at what had been my office door for years, but had to face the fact there was no point — it was Stephanie's office now. Andrea ignored me and checked through a desk diary to make an appointment for whoever was on the other end of the phone. I hovered for a few moments then took a seat. Not a barrel of laughs Alicia had said, but sharp and very efficient. Efficiency mightn't have been Janet's forte but she'd had a great sense of humor. I missed her already.

Alicia had time for a late lunch at Gino's, just around the corner. "Veetoria! You return already!" Gino kissed me on both cheeks and I apologized for not having looked up his cousin.

"It's all right, si. New York it is a big city and you are busy. You find yourself a boyfriend there?"

Gino and his wife Paola were ever-hopeful. And why shouldn't they be? Boyfriends hadn't been an item with Alicia, and then all of a sudden it's a full-blown wedding. Paola had done the catering. I pushed these thoughts away, ordered a vegetarian pizza, and graciously accepted the present of a free half bottle.

"Some things don't change." Alicia moved her bag so I could sit down.

"Pity Janet had to," I replied.

"Andrea is excellent, truly, you'll grow to love her."

"Uh huh. And is she going to love having me sitting in front of her desk all day? It could get a bit cramped out there you know. The clients'll be tripping over themselves and suing us for negligence."

"Meaning?"

I've never been able to decide whether Alicia is obtuse on purpose, or if it just comes naturally. "My office, Alicia — Stephanie inhabits my office and you said you were getting the builders in ... remember?"

"Of course I remember." She frowned and sawed at her pizza. "There's a women's building collective who are going to do it but they're a bit behind at the moment."

"Like the feminist roofers were? We spent three weeks emptying buckets."

"So there aren't many women around in these jobs and they get swamped."

"A pun I presume?"

"What? Oh." She didn't laugh.

"Okay, so my repartee's rotten. To be honest I'm not feeling remotely jokey."

"How *do* you feel?" Her eyes focused and she was back with me, concerned but businesslike.

"I feel like shit, I feel incompetent, I feel like I'm groping in the dark, I feel I'm missing something very obvious, I feel I'm putting April in danger." I wasn't after pity or reassurance, this was just a statement of fact.

"Right." She put down her fork and whipped out a notebook. "We'll go through this now, step by step. I've got an appointment at three, can you make dinner in Soho?"

"Yes." I had something planned for the afternoon myself.

"Good. I've got a surveillance to do, nothing heavy. We'll go over everything now and tonight we'll go over it all a second time." This was our usual way of dealing with problems, it felt good to be picking up on the routine again.

Three quarters of an hour later I bid goodbye to Gino, parted from Alicia at the corner, and set off in search of a bus. Another thirty minutes and, still clutching my *London A–Z*, I was walking towards a shop with a black and red sign, *Sacco & Vanzetti*. Polished floors, stripped pine, something classical playing in the background. The sections were labelled with typed cards reading *Feminism, Green Politics, New Age*. A tall man in jeans and a white shirt stacking books I identified at a glance as Will. Alicia was right, no way was this guy going to be seen dead in a woolly hat. I took a quick look and then turned back to *Gay Politics*. He finished what he was doing, then I felt him standing behind me.

"Can I help you?" He sounded friendly and good-humored.

"I'm looking for something for a friend, actually."

"Not April, by any chance?"

What? I swung round and stared at him.

Laughter lines crinkled around his hazel eyes. "She rang this morning to say she suspected you might be paying us a surprise visit and if you did would I offer you tea and introduce you to Gareth if he was home from school. Unfortunately he's not, but Jen's upstairs. Shall I put the sign on the door saying 'Gone to the revolution, back in thirty minutes'?"

He did put up the sign, and it really did say just that.

"Well, well," Alicia chuckled, "she has you sussed out, hasn't she?"

"Looks like it." In other circumstances I would have been laughing too, but these weren't other circumstances. Planning this afternoon's visit had allowed me to tell myself I was still in control, that there was still an investigation going on. But now that I had met them I had to admit I couldn't keep Will and Jen on my list — in fact they seemed as worried about April as I was.

"So here I am," I played with my fork, "back to square one."

"So here you are in a house of ill repute." She glanced around. "What I can't understand about this place, however, is why they bother with the sideline. I mean at the prices they pile on for the wine and the extras, how come they need to run a brothel as well? I came here a couple of months ago with

171

Stephanie and Andrea and the bill was sixty-five quid for two bottles of wine, three pizzas and three minuscule desserts. Can you believe that?"

"I find it hard to believe feminists eat out in brothels these days." Not that it looked like a brothel to me, all I could see was a small, shabby-looking pizzeria.

"We didn't know what it was till it got to eleven and they locked the door and started pulling the curtains, I'd just been told it was an 'interesting' place to eat late."

"They lock you in?" I didn't think I was in the mood.

"They lock new customers out, and pull the curtains round each table."

"They should be reported to the health inspectors." I leaned forward and stared suspiciously at the heavy maroon curtains, now discreetly at the end of their rails.

"Tacky isn't it?" Alicia beamed.

"Yeah." I didn't like the look of those curtains at all. "In every possible sense."

My guess was that for our waitress this was the equivalent of a night off. She was an old nineteen, heavily peroxided, her false eyelashes constantly in danger of joining the pizza toppings. There was no denying she knew her stuff though, and to my ears her Italian was flawless. Except for the fact that the man at the door had pimp written all over him the atmosphere was good-humored and relaxed, and the food really was excellent. Alicia asked for another candle and we spread lunchtime's notes across the table and went through it all again: the letters, the paint, the dead rat; the boy with blonde hair, his jugular severed.

The red of my dress clashed with the curtains. "I match their shop colors," I said.

"What, here?" Across from me Alicia was in navy blue, a businesswoman out for a taste of bohemia. Every so often she glanced at her watch; the man she was looking out for was due around ten.

"The book shop, anarchist red and black."

"Oh." She went back to chewing her pen, then sighed. "It's a waiting game, Tor, there's nothing else to be done. Either there's something going on that we know nothing about, or there's a complete nutter at large. I go for the first option. Nutters are usually fairly up-front." She leaned back and put down the pen. "You know what I really don't understand about all this? Why is it that her son hasn't been threatened yet? If they're really trying to freak April out, surely that would be the way to do it?"

"I've wondered about that too. I guess it's their trump card and they're keeping it till last." It was a grim prospect, and not something I wanted to dwell on. "Look, that's enough about my problems for tonight. What happens when this bloke arrives, by the way? You're not tailing him from here are you? I have to keep an eye on the train times."

"No, I just want to make sure this is where he comes."

"No bugs in the pizza? You're not wired?"

"He's not here for pizza, my guess is that he'll have a word with our friend at the door and will head up those back stairs."

"To the ladies loo?" I usually locate the loo sign fairly on, just to be on the safe side.

"The loos are on the first floor, the other amenities higher up. Why don't you go and powder your nose for ten minutes and I'll spend some time thinking about pudding."

I should have known. "Come on, Alicia, if you want the place looked at why don't you go?"

"Because I'm waiting for our man to walk through the door."

"And if I meet him on the staircase?"

"I'm sure he'll move aside to let you pass, I hear he's quite a gentleman. Go on, Tor, dinner's been on expenses."

I went to the loo first, which wasn't palatial but was scrupulously clean. I didn't powder my nose but did blot it with paper towels after which I used the cover-stick. A run through my hair with the comb, earrings still in place, dress looking good. I peed, dabbed at my nose again and then couldn't think of any more excuses.

What the heck — I opened the door out into the hall. It was dimly-lit, but the flowered carpet was newish and had recently been vacuumed. I took a deep breath and continued on up to the top floor.

"Love, are you lost or are you looking for someone?" She was wearing a flimsy pink gown over a black bra and knickers.

I giggled tipsily and sank onto the top step. "I guess we're all lost up here."

"You're right there." There were three doors. The one behind her was half-open and I could see a large bed with purple sheets, prettily lit by a pink table lamp.

174

"Is that your room?" I asked, innocent-cum-flirty. "I've always fancied colored sheets." I giggled again. "Are they — you know — are they hard to keep clean?"

She flirted straight back. "Do they show the stains you mean? Well it depends on what's been spilt on them. Only safe sex here, all my men friends wear a rubber. But with ladies, well that's different, those damp patches, they don't stain."

I smiled up at her and wondered how many women friends she had. A few probably, but they were unlikely to be paying customers. From the look she was giving me, my guess was that women counted as recreation. Unless, that is, they were potential customers like me, half-plastered so they could pretend they hadn't really meant it, while finding out if they really liked it.

"Catrina?"

"Here, Shona, having a chat on the stairs." She didn't take her eyes off me but managed to shrug her gown off one shoulder. Her neck and arms were unblemished except for a faint blue bruise that was strangely attractive on her white skin.

"Hi there honey, you waiting for Ruby or you just chatting here with Cat? You can come and chat with me if you like." Shona was tall and black in a white half slip. Her breasts were uncovered and she brazenly ran a finger across one nipple then laughed easily.

Catrina wasn't kidding however, she was for real. She slid down next to me on the step and put an arm loosely around my shoulders. "Ruby's busy with one of her sixty-year-olds, all paunch and no push, she sits on top of them and they kid themselves they're giving it to her real rough." She kept her eyes glued greedily to mine and slipped a finger into her mouth. "I like it better with women."

Shona wandered back to her room. "Don't let John-boy hear you say that honey, even though it is true!" She laughed again and shut her door.

The finger came out of Catrina's mouth and ran its tip along mine. "You game or not?" she said. I wanted the finger to slip between my lips, I wanted her to pull me up and take me into the room with the purple sheets.

Then the finger was in my mouth and she was saying, "You are sweet. You are young and sweet and I'm old enough to be your mother." Which was a lie, but the next thing she said was true. "I could hurt you, not much, but enough." I pushed her away and stood up unsteadily.

"I think I've come to the wrong floor." I smoothed my dress and she leaned lazily against the banisters.

"I don't think so, I think you know just where you are. And this is where I'll be when you decide to come back."

I smiled weakly and made my way back down the steps. Sorry Cat, but you only read me half right.

Alicia had ordered for both of us. "That was closer to fifteen than ten, I was beginning to think I was going to have to go up and rescue you."

"Me too."

"You weren't mistaken for one of the staff, were you? Some bloke with a limp prick tell you his wife doesn't understand him?"

"Not exactly." I could still feel the smooth finger against the tip of my tongue. Picking up my glass I carefully put my voice into neutral. "There are three women working the top floor. Catrina's white, Shona's black, I didn't get to see Ruby. The place looks clean, they don't seem doped, I didn't catch sight of any obvious needle marks and it's a safe-sex establishment."

"What did you do, ask to read their literature?" Alicia sounded pleased. She glanced to the door and then back at me. "Our friend has just arrived, take a look."

He was fiftyish, well-dressed, typical City.

"And he likes black women, so I think it's safe to assume he's on his way upstairs to visit Shona. Right, that's us done. Coffee followed by the bill? Thank God this isn't going to be another late night."

I didn't ask for the details. Alicia's views on divorce work have always been somewhat different from mine.

CHAPTER NINETEEN

Bruised petals, bruised clouds: I stretched out under the copper beech and let my gaze fall from cloud to tree to yellow hair to blue, blue eyes. It was Easter Monday. Yesterday we'd taken a walk in the University Parks, swinging round the spiked gates into the grounds of Magdalen, where we'd followed Addison's Walk to the seclusion of the Fellows' Garden. In the afternoon it had rained and I'd borrowed one of April's sweaters and we'd snuggled close and read and drunk coffee and finished a bottle of wine. Dinner had been fingers of toast and soft boiled eggs.

Today was sunny again. "The last day of April." My April trailed a piece of grass across my mouth. "You know what that means?"

"It means it's the anniversary of Hitler's suicide in the bunker." I must have picked that up from Alicia somewhere along the line.

"It means that pretty soon we'll have known each other for a whole month. You know it feels longer, it feels like I've known you for years."

"Yes, well, quite a lot has happened." I wasn't too keen on the counting business — we'd agreed on ten days of April keeping company with Blade and there wasn't long to go.

"We only know each other in Oxford. I'm going to fall in love with you all over again when I meet your London self. What will you look like in London, Victoria?"

"You'll recognize me by the high heels and shoulder pads. Oh yes, and I also wear a wig — short and curly."

"Yummy, I'll adore you in a wig."

In fact I do sometimes resort to the wig but I don't look yummy at all. April, however, would have to discover this for herself.

Getting out of bed well before dawn isn't something that would appeal to me at the best of times. But getting out of bed so as to have a strawberry and champagne breakfast with a woman who disliked me intensely — in other words Jo — was adding insult to injury.

"I won't," I said, my eyes shut tightly against the light. "I know it's May Day and all that but I won't."

"That's okay, don't you come if you don't want to," April chirped. "I'm quite happy to walk all the way to Magdalen Bridge by myself ... In the dark."

It took about three seconds for that to sink in. Four seconds later I rolled out of bed in time to see April pick up her towel and head for the bathroom.

The day was cold but at least it wasn't raining. All along the road there were groups of two and three, sometimes more. Deborah and April kept up a steady chatter. I sulked. We met Jo and Blade at the Martyr's Memorial and the five of us then walked along Broad Street and New College Lane before joining a slow-moving river of people that completely filled the end of the High.

"How you doing, Tor?" Blade called, her left arm linked securely through April's right.

I nodded at her and watched the people around us, a mixture of youth and age, but mainly youth. A lot of students had come back early for this and there were young women in mini skirts, in ball gowns; young men in jeans and evening dress. In the gates of the various colleges musicians tuned their instruments and tested their sound equipment. Dotted throughout the crowd were the inevitable Morris dancers.

April nudged me. "There's Ali from the co-op. She's in a women's Morris group. Only one problem."

"What's that?"

"Have a look at what she's wearing. The skirt's okay but they insist on T-shirts and most of them don't wear bras, you can see the audience's eyes all going up, down, up, down, it's riveting!" Before I could reply there was a surge from behind and we found ourselves actually on the bridge. I didn't particularly fancy standing on a bridge designed for the load of everyday traffic with a couple of thousand other people, but I guessed this event had been happening for a few hundred years and it hadn't collapsed so far. There is, of course, always a first time.

I said, "Are you sure it's safe?"

April shook her head. "No. That's half the fun!"

After a general looking at watches, the crowd began to settle. Gradually there was silence and within a couple of minutes a chorus of golden voices floated down from Magdalen's crenelated tower. Up above us we could just make out the small figures of the boys in their black and white surplices and, beyond them, an apricot sky turning blue. The stone of the tower flushed warm as honey and a seagull called from somewhere above, its voice mingling with the medieval hymn to the sun. And then it was over. There was a brief, still, silence and then the mood changed to laughter and a volley of champagne corks. The partying had begun.

"This way." Jo pointed to the right and we gradually moved to that side of the road until we finally made it onto the pavement and then cut up along Catte Street and into Radcliffe Square. A Morris circle was already underway in front of the Radcliffe Camera while in the shadow of St. Mary's an alternative Punch and Judy was being watched by a crowd who shouted, "*That's* the way to do it!" every time the protagonists kissed.

Not all the elements of the crowd were so right-on, however, and from above the sound of the bands in the High there came occasional shouts and at one stage a smashing of glass that suggested a shop window had met with a nasty accident. We watched the dancers for a while and then decided it was time for strawberries and made our way back into the High again. Here things were louder and more drunken. On the roof of University College two young men wearing clown masks frolicked with their jeans around their ankles. Every so often they pulled their pants down too, presenting their bums to the street. There were whistles and cat-calls and someone threw a bottle which smashed half-way up the wall. We pushed back in the direction of the bridge and suddenly there were yells in front and a surge out from what appeared to be a shishkebab van. A woman screamed and the roof of the van seemed to sway.

"Can you see?" I yelled at Jo.

She raised herself up on Blade's shoulder. "They're pushing it over!"

We couldn't move in any direction, we were held by the pressure of the crowd. Then we found ourselves shoved even nearer. I stood on my toes to see.

Two men, one on either side, were rocking the van to and fro. The black driver was trapped inside, the fat from the deep fryer splashing in a wavelike motion from one side to the other in front of him.

The man opened his mouth in a silent scream and then leapt for the door as his vehicle slowly arced into the middle of the road. Amid shouts, one of the men disappeared into the crowd while the other briefly turned towards us, his right hand raised in a fascist salute. He wore a leather jacket and his head was shaved; on his forehead I could make out a tattoo.

Blade grabbed my arm. "Is it him?"

I pushed a startled April in the direction of Jo and Deborah. "Take April straight to your flat! Get her away from here!"

The salute disappeared up ahead and Blade and I battled after it.

We weren't the only ones in pursuit. There were cries of anger as people realized what had happened and someone yelled, "Stop him! Somebody stop him!" No one did.

We forced our way through the crowd and down a narrow lane which skirted the Botanic Gardens and led in the direction of Christ Church Meadow. Ahead the skin dashed toward a gate and then suddenly he wasn't running anymore but trying to scale the fence: the meadow was still locked.

A man flung himself at the ascending legs, there was a flurry of hands and boots and then it was all over. Our quarry was huddled in a swearing heap at the bottom of the iron railings while we stood over him in a circle, gasping our exhaustion in unison. There was a very brief, oh-so-civilized conference and someone went off to get the police.

Blade shook her head and pulled a face. "I'm glad we caught him," she muttered to me, "but it's a pity he isn't Prince." I'd shown her the photo at the beginning of the week and she was right, he was a skin and he had a tattoo, but he wasn't Prince.

CHAPTER TWENTY

April was very restrained while we were still at Jo and Blade's, she didn't yell at me once. Blade and I arrived to find the strawberries waiting, the cream whipped, the champagne chilled. Blade enthusiastically related the chase and April calmly smiled and served breakfast. When we got home she let rip.

"What the fuck did you think you were up to? Was that meant to be *macho* or something, treating me like some piece of china while you go racing off

185

after some Nazi psychopath? Enough is enough, you're acting like you're going crazy! And if you're not crazy *I* soon will be at this rate!"

She slammed downstairs to the kitchen and I lay on the bed and thought over the events of the past week: me hiding among the garbage bags, turning up at the bookshop, dining out at a brothel. She was right, my life had taken on a sense of the bizarre. But the macho jibe was bloody unfair.

We spent a quiet afternoon, both taking care to give the other space. Deborah and April took blankets and books out onto the lawn and I cycled round to Rosemary and Eleanor's, just to say hello and to check for messages. When I got back I looked out the window and Deborah and April were still there, still reading. I sat on the edge of the desk and absently leafed through a pile of April's essays. *Consideration as a Problem: Discuss. Is English Land Law Nothing but the Feudal System Writ Large?* I wondered who was responsible for the diabolical titles. Despite the unpromising subject matter, however, April had scored beta plus for one, alpha minus for the other. Not only was the lady beautiful, she was bright.

I picked up the land law essay and read the first paragraph, rubbing my right thumb down the edge of the page — there were no perforations and the edges hadn't been torn off, the paper size was eleven inch. I flipped through the pile to the more recent work. Here the paper was larger A4, the edges neatly removed.

Mechanically I got up and went downstairs to the kitchen to collect the key that hung out of sight on a nail in one of the cupboards. I walked down the hall, past April's old room, and unlocked the door to

the computer room, then locked it again behind me.
There were two word processors and two dot matrix
printers. I checked the paper in each. It was A4,
with perforated edges. I switched on the nearest
machine, putting in the start-of-day disk which was
sitting on the table. I moved the cursor to the
template entry and then went into edit. A couple of
minutes later I created a document and printed a
couple of words: both the print and the template
matched the layout of April's essays.

They also matched the letters I'd read in
Eleanor's office.

"Hi, back already?" She dropped the blanket on
the floor and came over to kiss me. "Forgiven me
yet?"

"What for?"

"For giving you an earful this morning."

"For that I forgive you completely."

"Blade rang to say she overdosed on strawberries
and she mightn't be able to come to the library with
me tomorrow." Her eyes didn't meet mine, "I know
we agreed on ten days, but I think eight's enough,
don't you?"

"More than enough."

"So you agree then?" She sounded surprised, and
relieved. "You think I'm safe?"

"Yes, I really do, April."

She whistled happily as she sorted out the
papers on her desk and I watched her and cursed
myself for having been so stupid. I hadn't understood
what was going on at all.

* * * * *

The next morning I rang Phoebe at nine o'clock. She was still in bed and not very happy at having been woken up.

"I'm sorry Pheebes, but this is important, I really need to talk."

"Hey, you and April haven't had a bust up have you?"

"No we haven't but it is important."

She yawned and thought for a moment. "I'll tell you what, you need to talk and I could do with a bit of exercise to get rid of some of the flab, so let's take a short cycle ride to the Perch. How about I meet you at the lodge at eleven?

I'd been hoping she'd say in five minutes. "Great. See you then."

I whiled away the time at College, mechanically working straight onto the Amstrad. Some *investigator* I thought, some archivist, if it came to that. The evidence had all been there, staring me in the face, and I'd simply looked right through it. So madly in love I couldn't think straight, so much in love I'd ignored all my training, all my experience.

"How's it going?" Rosemary asked as she walked in.

"Fine. Thanks."

"Your friend Sarah rang. She apologizes but says no luck."

"Right. Oh well, it's good to know she's still working on it."

It could prove useful if she did track Prince down, but it was no longer urgent.

At a quarter to eleven I finished what I was

doing and told Rosemary I mightn't be able to come in for a couple of days but would catch up on any lost time as soon as I could. She said that wasn't a problem and didn't ask for the whys or wherefores.

"I thought we were going to the Perch?"

Phoebe had cycled to the end of Binsey Lane, past the sign pointing to the pub. Now she was chaining her bike up in front of a church. "First a pilgrimage, although it being May we've left things late."

The fact I didn't know what she was on about must have been writ large on my uncomprehending face.

"Chaucer's Prologue," she said condescendingly. "Come on, Tor, think back to those A-levels. 'Whan that Aprill with hise shoures soote, The droghte of March hath perced to the roote ... Thanne longen folk to go on pilgrimages.' No?" She sighed. "Secure your bike, then follow me."

When I caught up with her she was on her knees, reaching down into a small, dingy well with an empty jar.

"What on earth are you doing?"

"Oh, Tor!" She looked deeply disappointed, which was the sort of look I felt I deserved. "This is *it*, the Dormouse's treacle well from *Alice in Wonderland*. Old Charles certainly knew his stuff — 'treacle' is a pun you see, it's an obsolete word for medicinal or healing."

Treacle. I felt as if my mind had been swimming in it. "And the jam jar?"

189

"I'm collecting water for my elderly next door neighbor, who's Russian Orthodox — the Free Church in Exile I hasten to add, not the lot that she insists are still run by the K.G.B. Anyway, every few months she asks me to fill up on holy water for her. You *do* know the story of our patron saint don't you?" I didn't even have to shake my head, she just assumed ignorance and continued, "About 700 A.D. a randy Saxon king named Algar put the hard word on Frideswide, when all she wanted to do was be a nun. Divine justice was meted out and he was blinded for his presumption. She eventually forgave him and cured him with water from this well. He, of course, was converted on the spot."

Blinded by lust, I could relate to that.

She sat up again and held the jar to the light. The water inside was filthy.

"I hope the old lady's not going to drink it."

"Nah, she boils it and sprinkles it on stuff."

"On her food? It looks like it needs more than a boil."

"On people. It keeps away demons, which is hardly surprising. Pretty rancid eh?"

We wheeled our bikes back to the Perch and took our glasses and packets of crisps to a secluded table in the far corner of the garden.

"Orange juice?" She wrinkled her nose at my glass. "I thought this was soul-baring time."

"This isn't soul-baring, it's fact-gathering. I haven't been thinking clearly for the past month. In fact I'm tempted to give up the booze altogether."

"Teetotal? This all sounds terribly earnest."

"It is," I said. "Deadly earnest. I've been thinking about something you said weeks ago, the night of

Rosemary and Eleanor's sherry party. We were outside and I'd just met April."

"Uh huh." She slowly tore open a packet of crisps. "And I'd just met Malcolm."

"That's right, and you were talking to April about how she got her room in the house, do you remember? You said the rumor was that Damian had been dealing. What do you know about that?"

She gave me an odd look. "So this is what it's like talking to a private detective? You must understand I don't know anything for sure, I don't use the stuff myself. But among the fast set, in other words the undergraduates with money, word was that it was Damian you bought your coke from — some said ecstasy too, and crack. When he suddenly disappeared gossip had it that his father had twigged and hauled him straight onto the next flight to the States. His father's American and he and Damian's mother live there most of the time. Damian and his sister had their own flat in a rather nice part of London, Kensington I think. Convenient for Harrods."

"Do you know if anyone's seen Damian recently?"

"I don't think so, my guess is that he's playing office boy somewhere and that Daddy's keeping him on a very short leash."

"Okay, you said Damian was in some sort of student club?"

"A *dining* society please, very posh, very nasty. They have a history of wrecking rooms that have been hired out to them and abusing the staff."

"Do you know if Antony's in the same club? How close were they?"

Phoebe rested her chin on her hands. "Look, I'm

not part of that group, Tor. I can only tell you what the gossip was. As far as I know they were very close, and much of a muchness if you ask me. Damian was an arrogant little shit, Antony's more charming but I suspect he's just as unpleasant at heart. Socializing in that set is all about passing the port in the right direction, in other words to the left, and throwing up on the table later so that some low-paid minion has to clear it up. I told you about their famous dinner party where they hired a skinhead couple to fuck on the table, didn't I? I've heard that was Antony's idea. I don't know if it's true but that's what people said at the time."

"Phoebe," I said, "you've told me all I ever needed to know."

CHAPTER TWENTY-ONE

Rosemary hesitated, looked at my face, then picked up the phone and rang the College Secretary, who quickly came up with Damian's London address and telephone number. I put my hand out for the phone and she left the room.

The number was dead. I tried directory assistance and was told there was a new number, unlisted. At which I immediately rang the agency and asked for Alicia.

Andrea said she was out for most of the day, could she help? I outlined the problem and she said she'd get back to me within the half hour. She was as good as her word, and she had the number.

"Thank you." I was more than grateful.

"No problem at all," she replied coolly. "Anything else and I'll see what I can do." She hung up and I started dialing.

"Hello, is that Susannah?" Around the receiver my knuckles were white while my voice, I hoped, oozed a friendly American accent.

"Who is this?"

"My name's Cheryl Stallman." My mind briefly conjured up the image of a woman I'd met once at a dinner party somewhere, sometime. "My mother knows a friend of a friend of your mother, you know how it is!" Hopefully this would explain how it was I had an unlisted number. "Anyway I've just arrived over here and I'm looking for a nice area to live in in London and Mom suggested I should meet you and ask for your advice. I mean, some of these apartments sound keen but for all I know they could be in the Bronx! I have to find somewhere real soon and I was sort of wondering if I could visit tomorrow morning." I feared this didn't sound very convincing, my American isn't that good at the best of times.

Susannah, however, didn't seem to notice. "I'm sorry but I'm afraid I can't see you tomorrow, and I don't think I'd be able to give you that sort of advice anyway. You could try the company we lease this flat from — they're very good. I'm sure they'll be able to help." She reeled off a central London number.

"Oh that's great, thank you. Maybe we could have a drink anyway, Susannah. To tell you the truth I'm a bit lonely, I came over here to be with my boyfriend but I'm not sure things are going to work out. I'd really like to talk it over with someone. You doing anything tonight?"

"I'm sorry but I am," she said quickly. "I'm going out to dinner. And tomorrow I'm going away for a while."

"Oh that's nice. You going on holiday or on business? Maybe we could meet when you get back?"

"I'm going on a long holiday." By now she sounded slightly frantic. "I've only just finished packing and now I have to go and collect my ticket, I still have heaps to do and I'll be out all day." There was the sound of a doorbell in the background. "Look Shirley . . ."

"Cheryl, Cheryl Stallman. My mother met your . . ."

"The cleaning woman's arrived so I have to go. I hope everything works out for you, Cheryl, goodbye!"

Shit. Was she just trying to get rid of a potential nuisance or was she really going away? I rang Andrea again. "I know Alicia's not there," I said, "but this is urgent. Could you ask Stephanie if she could fit it in? I have to know if this woman is leaving the country, and when."

"Stephanie's not here today." Andrea's voice was non-committal. "But I'll see what I can do for you. Can you give me the address?"

My eyelid twitched fiercely. If Andrea blundered in, Susannah might get suspicious, but I had to find out if she really was about to leave. There wasn't any choice.

"Fine," she said after I'd explained as tactfully as possible that this had to be handled like glass. "Will you still be at the same number later this afternoon?"

I told her I'd be back at the house, gave her that number, and set off for home.

Half an hour later the phone rang. Sarah's voice greeted me. "I spoke to your aunt this morning and said I hadn't any news, but after lunch I tried Prince's Mum again and she says the boy wonder has sent a postcard from Amsterdam saying he's having a massive time. He's headed back to his old haunts. I'll get onto my contacts there and ask them to keep an eye out, okay?"

"Okay. Thanks, Sarah." Prince was still a witness, after all.

"How things going your end?" She was settling down for a chat.

"I'm not sure — but busy. Look, I'm expecting a call so I have to go. I'll be in touch."

"I understand. Good luck." She rang off.

Andrea was back on the line an hour later. I said as calmly as I could, "Have you come up with anything?"

"Have you got a pen?"

"Yes." I dropped it and chased it under my chair while she kept talking.

"She's booked on an Air Italia flight to Rome tomorrow, leaving Heathrow seven pm. She's packed her stuff and has gone out for the rest of the day. She'll be spending the night with her boyfriend in his Hampstead flat. She'll collect her luggage sometime tomorrow, she'll probably come round in a taxi and her boyfriend will then collect her to go to the airport. She has an open ticket which is valid for twelve months but she's expecting to be away about three."

There was only one thing to say to that and I said it. "Thank you."

"I used to know a lot of the women who did cleaning round there, my grandmother was one of them for about fifteen years. It was quite possible that I'd know this woman too, so I simply knocked on the door."

"And it was someone you knew!"

"No, she isn't Afro-Caribbean, she's Spanish. I said I was looking for work and Graciela was very sympathetic and enjoyed having a talk. The poor woman's lost a hefty slice of her income at twenty-four hours' notice — Miss Susannah's told her that she only wants her to come in once a week to water the plants. Up till now she's been there three times a week, doing the washing and ironing and even providing a few meals. She's got to find herself some more work this week."

"It sounds as if Susannah's made a snap decision."

"Seems so. She had a good job with an advertising agency and she's ditched them with the same amount of notice. Graciela said her boss has rung several times hopping mad. Her parents aren't too pleased either, Daddy's messages on the answer machine have been something else."

"Did Graciela know if Susannah's brother Damian was somehow involved in this?"

"She said Susannah's brother was in New York and that a message had come from him while she was there yesterday afternoon. All he said was that he was really sorry. She doesn't know what's going on but Susannah's seemed depressed for a couple of weeks, looks scared, jumps at the drop of a pin. Graciela thinks she's having some sort of breakdown."

"I can't thank you enough for this, I couldn't have asked for more."

"If you do think of anything else," she said briskly, "just let me know."

I spent the next hour or so with my feet up on the sofa, doing some heavy thinking. Eventually I went through to the kitchen, poured myself some apple juice, then sat down to ring Andrea again. She listened to my latest request and replied she couldn't foresee any problems, she'd expect me in the office shortly after eight tomorrow morning.

I started apologizing about the early start. "There's no need," she cut in, "I'm usually here by eight."

CHAPTER TWENTY-TWO

The seven o'clock train got me into London at seven-fifty and I was at Andrea's desk fifteen minutes after she was. I'd spent an hour on the phone to Alicia the previous night. She emerged from her office when she heard me arrive.

"What is this?" I asked. "Are you making eight o'clock starts as well?"

She yawned. "Steph and I have to meet a client at nine and we need to compare notes first." She kissed me on both cheeks. I kissed her back.

In the background Andrea was dangling some car

keys. "It's a gray Saab, which blends in suitably with the local scenery. It's parked two doors west of Susannah's block, on the opposite side of the road. You can't miss it but here's the number in case. It's got a disabled parking permit and you can sit there all day if you like."

"I don't suppose anyone could come and relieve me in a few hours' time?" Because I knew that in a few hours' time I'd be desperate to pee.

"How about I come by at eleven?" Alicia asked. "If Susannah hasn't made an appearance by two, you can give Andrea a call and she'll come over. That all right with you?"

She was asking Andrea, not me. Andrea nodded and held out a mobile phone. "Make it five past," she said. "I'll just be getting back from lunch."

I was at South Kensington tube by quarter to nine and sitting in the Saab by nine on the dot. If you're going to spend possibly all day cooped up in a car watching the passersby you don't want it to be too warm, or you'll doze off, nor do you want it to rain so that everyone's hidden under umbrellas. Today, inevitably, it was spitting during the walk from the tube, but as soon as I'd climbed into the passenger's seat the clouds cleared. An hour later I'd counted eight mink coats, despite the clement weather.

Just before eleven Alicia opened the door. "On the muggy side, isn't it?" She held out a King Cone. I slid over into the driver's seat and she sat down next to me. "There's a particularly nasty wine bar just round that corner where you can get yourself a drink and use the loo."

"Thanks, Alicia."

"I couldn't have you melting away."

"Thanks for everything, not just the ice cream. I'll pay you back I promise, just send me the bill for the car hire and everything else."

"Forget it, there's no need for that and you know it. Now scoot and stretch your legs. Don't forget the phone — if she arrives I'll call."

Susannah didn't arrive in the twenty minutes I was away. Alicia sat with me for a while and then went back to the agency. I tried ignoring my aching back and started counting couples in which the man was a good twenty years older than his female companion: I'd soon beaten the record for minks. Alicia had also brought me some sandwiches and by two o'clock I'd finished them and there was still no sight of Susannah. I rang Andrea.

"Tor here. Can you give me a break or are you snowed under?"

"We're always snowed under but Stephanie and Alicia are both in, so it's okay. I'll see you in about half an hour."

When I got back from the wine bar for the second time Andrea was wearing sunglasses. "I saw Graciela up at the corner," she explained, "and didn't want her to recognize me. She'd wonder what I was up to. Maybe you should go up and see her, she might have got a message from Susannah saying when she's coming."

She got out of the car. I thought about it for a few minutes and then decided to take her advice.

There were about twelve names listed by the door. I pushed the button under Susannah's and the security phone crackled into life.

"Yes?"

"Hi there," I cooed into the grill. "I've come to see Susannah."

"She is not here now."

"What was that? I'm sorry but I can't hear you."

"Miss Susannah not here now."

"Oh that's real disappointing. My name's Cheryl Stallman. I spoke to Susannah on the phone yesterday morning and she said she was going away today but as I was in the neighborhood I thought I'd call in case she hadn't left yet."

"She has not left yet but she is not here."

"At least I can leave her my number. Can you open the door please? I haven't got a pen with me here."

"You come in the lift to the second floor." There was another crackle and then the door clicked open.

Letter boxes lined the wall immediately on the left but they didn't seem to be in use. Beyond the inner glass doors there was a low marble table with neat piles of mail. At a glance I couldn't see anything for Susannah but Graciela would have collected it already. I pushed the button for the lift, slid the metal grill aside and stepped in.

Graciela was polite but not forthcoming, so there was no way I'd be able to emulate Andrea's achievements of yesterday.

"My Mom will be real sorry when she hears I missed Susannah," I said. "Is there any chance she might be back soon?"

She shrugged. "I do not know when she will be here. I am sorry I cannot help you, but I have much work to do now. You leave your telephone number, si?" As she held out a pen and note pad, I could see three grey suitcases behind her.

I scrawled something illegible, signed it Cheryl, topped off with a smiley face, and added an imaginary phone number.

"Goodbye then, and thank you."

"Goodbye." She quickly shut the door.

Graciela left the building shortly after four o'clock. I hunched down into the seat and was only just re-emerging when a black taxi pulled up in front of the flats. Susannah's hair was longer than in Deborah's photo but I recognized her all the same. I jumped out of the car and ran up the front steps.

"Thanks!" I said breathlessly, slipping in behind her. "That saves me searching for my keys."

She nodded vaguely and walked over to the lift. I took the stairs two at a time. Hearing her door click shut as I got to the top, I stood back against the wall wondering whether to knock or wait. Then the door opened and she came out lugging two of the cases.

I stepped forward and reached out my hand. "Can I help you with one of those?"

Under her makeup she lost all her color. "You gave me a shock."

"Did I? I'm sorry. One good turn deserves another and you saved me looking for my key so when I saw you coming out with your cases I thought I should offer to do you a favor in return."

She smiled faintly. "Thank you, but I can manage. I'll put these in the lift."

"Fine, I'll hold the door for you."

"Oh, yes ..." She hesitated for a moment then turned and walked back into the room for the third case. I stepped in behind her, shut the door and leaned against it.

Her eyes were wide, she was scared stiff. "I'm fine," she stammered. "I really don't need your help ..."

"I know that," I said, "but I need yours. I don't know who you're frightened of, Susannah, but it's not me. I'm not here to hurt you but I am here to make sure no one else does get hurt. I have to talk to you about your brother."

"No!" She shook her head, tears already beginning to run down her face. She really was on the edge. "I won't tell you anything!"

"You will," I said gently. "I'm a private detective and I'm involved in this because a very good friend of mine has been threatened too. I'm not working for the police but if you don't help me I'll have to go to them. When's your boyfriend coming to pick you up?"

"Soon," she said desperately. "Simon will be here very soon!"

"Good, we'd better get this over quickly then, hadn't we?"

Susannah had slumped onto the sofa and I sat on a chair opposite. "You and your mother packed up his room. Did you know there were drugs hidden in it?"

I held my breath, I was banking everything on my guess being right. It was.

"No." She looked blankly at the wall ahead. "I knew Damian had been using drugs — that's why Daddy was making him leave Oxford. But I didn't know he'd been dealing, or that he had any hidden. I didn't know that until a few weeks ago."

"How did you find out? Was it from the person who's been frightening you?"

She reached into her pocket for a tissue. "A man rang and said that Damian had something that belonged to him — some cocaine — and if I didn't find out where it was he'd do something to my face. I rang Damian in New York that night. He told me there was a packet of drugs hidden behind the plywood at the back of the wardrobe in his College room."

"Did the man ring again? Did you tell him this?"

"Yes, he rang the next day and I told him."

"Have you heard from him again, Susannah?"

She nodded, her face crumpling. "He rang again, he said he hadn't been able to find a way of getting into the house and that I had to go and get the drugs for him. He said I'd be able to get into the house because I'm Damian's sister."

"But you didn't want to do that?"

"No! I told him that Damian and I could give him money, but he said that wasn't what he wanted, he wanted the cocaine." And then she wailed. "Please, I think I'm going to be sick."

She wasn't. I asked her where the booze was kept and poured her a brandy instead.

"I know this is frightening," I told her, "and that's why it's got to stop. You'll be safe in Italy but there are other people here who might get hurt."

She nodded. She didn't realize someone had already been killed and I didn't intend to tell her.

"I want to talk to you now about Antony."

Her whole body stiffened at his name.

"Susannah," I asked gently, "is he the person who's threatening you?"

"No."

"Are you sure?"

"Of course it's not him!" For the first time she sounded angry. "I'd recognize his voice."

Antony could be getting someone else to make the calls, but I didn't pursue that with her. "He and Damian used to be very close friends, didn't they? Do you think he knew about the drugs?"

"I'm sure he did, they were best friends for years."

"Okay, now I want you to think about this carefully. I know you went out with Antony for a while so you must have some idea of what sort of person he really is. He's great fun on the surface, Susannah, but what's he really like? Could he hurt someone?"

Her face contorted but she managed to keep control. "Yes," she whispered, "he could." She sat still for a moment and then slowly lifted her hands to the front of her blouse. I watched as she shakily undid the buttons. "Do you see?" she asked, giving a twisted smile.

A livid scar ran across the top of both breasts.

"What did he do to you?" I asked, appalled. "Did he cut you?"

"He burned me with a cigarette, while I was drunk. I can remember him saying something about ice and fire, and then I passed out. He sometimes arranged these parties with videos that someone got for him in Amsterdam. Everybody else seemed to think they were tremendous but I just drank to blot them out." She shook her head. "He said the next morning that he didn't mean to hurt me — and you know, I think he really meant it. Antony doesn't mean to hurt people, he just does whatever he happens to want to do at the time. I showed Damian what Antony had done to me and they had a fight."

She washed her face under the cold tap and I helped her with her suitcases. Simon came in the front door as we got out of the lift and as soon as he saw her face, he put both arms around her protectively. I left them to it.

I ate dinner with Alicia; Paul was still at work.

". . . And so," I summed up, "that was my day."

"It's a good thing she's out of it at any rate." Alicia sighed and leaned back against her chair.

"She should be okay in Italy for now. I feel guilty about lying but I had to persuade her to talk."

"It's not your fault. That boy was murdered and the police have to be told. If her brother stays in the States they mightn't slap a drugs charge on him. Serve him right if they do, anyway."

"That leaves Antony. A simple sadist or a murdering psychopath to boot? He's behind the threats against April, there's no doubt about that. My guess is that he knew Damian had the drugs hidden somewhere in his room, and realized Susannah and her mother wouldn't have packed them along with his undies."

"So he was desperate to search for them." Alicia topped up my wine. My brain was racing on alcohol and adrenalin. "And in order to take the room apart properly he had to get rid of April for longer than just a night or a weekend."

"That's right." I reached past the debris for a piece of brie. "He offered to swap rooms but she declined so he launched a campaign of harassment. He knew she'd found the first year difficult in various ways and he was hoping he'd be able to push her into leaving."

"He's nasty," she said, "but not very bright. How did he get into Oxford in the first place?"

"The right family, the right school, the right cheekbones, these little things help."

"Don't they ever."

"April was bearing up," I said, "so he started getting heavier. Enter Prince ..."

"Followed by a white rat."

"And now comes the difficult bit. Antony knew April was away, he thought her room would be empty. Either Antony went down to search yet again and killed the boy ..."

"Or there's a very frustrated dealer out there who had also found out April was away. He dropped by to collect his goods from behind the wardrobe, was surprised by Erich, killed him and ran off, *without* the drugs."

"Hence the demand that Susannah make a visit to the house." I could feel my whole body relax, the pieces were in place. "That's it, isn't it?" I said. "There has to be a third party. It's not just Antony."

"But Antony's vicious all the same, love. For Christ's sake don't forget that."

I got back to Oxford on the last train and quietly let myself in the front door. Luckily there was no sign of life from down the hall: I'd have time to decide how to handle Antony tomorrow morning.

April was waiting up for me. "I've been worried," she said.

"I'm sorry sweetheart." I bent and kissed her. "I love you."

"I love you, too." She pulled me down onto the bed.

Later she told me about her day. I'd already said mine would keep, and she didn't press me.

"So Blade's feeling better?"

"She's fine, and Deborah's hair, Tor — what a difference! She's thrilled, it really suits her. Oh yes, get this — I had tea with Mrs. Harvey and she claims Antony's acting very strangely. She reckons he's been pulling up the floorboards in his room! Do you think he's going quietly bonkers?"

I was feeling immensely weary. "I don't know about that, but I do happen to know he's been wasting his time."

CHAPTER TWENTY-THREE

Tomorrow morning came rather earlier than I'd expected.

"Tor!"

Catrina was flicking a lolly-pink whip and I was trying to tell her that she'd better stop because I was expecting my great aunt to arrive any minute now.

"Victoria, wake up!"

The whip vanished as the bedside lamp came on. "What? What is it?" I couldn't see a thing.

"Shh, listen."

I couldn't hear anything either. "What's the matter?"

"I heard someone."

That woke me up all right. Dear God, I'd forgotten the bolts!

April grabbed me as I jumped up to clamber out of bed. "Keep still and listen. Not up here, downstairs."

I sat listening to my own loud breathing. And then I heard it, two or three muffled thuds from the room below.

April suddenly giggled and relaxed. "It's Antony. He *is* taking up the floorboards."

To me it sounded more like he was moving an excessively heavy piece of furniture, the wardrobe for example. Fuck it, what to do now? I didn't fancy the thought of cornering him, even if there were two of us. I couldn't be one hundred percent sure he wasn't the one who'd knifed Erich. But could I risk waiting until tomorrow? What if he found the cocaine now and simply walked out with it? I wanted some proof.

Another thud from downstairs, followed this time by raised voices and two harsh screams. Antony had company and wasn't enjoying it. I was out of bed and grabbing for both gowns. "Look, we have to be bloody careful — these are the people who killed Erich. Keep behind me and if I say run, *run*."

She was white but managed to nod encouragement as I opened the door.

"April! Tor! Please!" Deborah stumbled down the stairs to join us. Bloody hell, we were forming a posse. "Please wait for me."

What to do with her? "When we get downstairs," I whispered, "I want you to ring the police. Stay in the phone room, Debs, and don't come out till we tell you."

The stairs were illuminated by a night light and the three of us crept quietly but quickly down. We froze in unison at the bottom, but no more sounds came from Antony's room. I nodded and Deborah tiptoed across the entrance hall in the direction of the phone.

I tugged at April's sleeve. "To the bathroom."

"What?" she hissed back.

"Follow me."

All I could think of was that we might be about to meet someone with a knife; a couple of towels would make me feel marginally safer. The bathroom door was open but it was pitch black inside. I crept forward, praying I wasn't about to trip over anything, and desperately ignoring the fact that what I wanted to do most in the world at this moment was pee. My hand touched something damp. One, two, three towels — that would be enough.

"Take this." I pushed a towel at her. "Wrap it around your right hand and arm as protection."

I did the same then picked up the third towel in my left hand. In theory you hold your right arm up as a shield and use the free towel to blind your attacker. In practice it was something I had yet to try. I wasn't looking forward to it.

Everything was silent as we moved down the hall towards Antony's door, taking short, light steps close against the wall, where the floorboards were less likely to creak. When we reached the door I stood between it and April and spent a whole ten seconds figuring out the best course of action.

"We've rung the police and they'll be here in a minute!" I yelled at the top of my lungs.

"What are you doing?" April was shocked into yelping from behind. "We want to surprise them."

Well she might. Me — I just wanted them to vacate the room.

Ignoring any fleeting desire to appear courageous I hammered on the door for good measure. "The police are here and we're coming in!" I turned the handle to dramatically fling the door open, only to find it was locked.

"Shit!"

"The window in the television room." April pointed down the hall. "That will be quicker. Come on!"

As I followed her I hoped whoever it was was over the garden wall by now.

I switched on a table lamp and April opened a window. There was no one in sight. We clambered out onto the grass then stood and listened. Nothing. I led the way, walking parallel with the back wall of the house. Antony's French doors were open, a light on inside. There was a faint grunting sound from within. I took a deep breath, a firm grip on both towels, and ducked my head past the green curtains.

There was some blood, yes, but nothing to compare with Deborah's description of what things had been like two weeks ago. And where the blood then had already dried into brown pools, here it was still crimson and flowing, or trickling rather, down Antony's bare back.

"Antony?"

He turned quickly and gave a sharp yelp. The

knife-man had gone, Antony was hurt but he wasn't about to bleed to death. I heaved a huge sigh of relief and realized my legs were shaking. It served the bastard right. Behind me April was more sympathetic.

"Antony!" She hurried round the end of the bed. "You're all right Antony, we're here and the police are coming."

She didn't know it of course but that wasn't likely to make Antony feel a whole lot better.

"So who's been using you to play naughts-and-crosses on, then?" I unwrapped the towel from around my right hand and looked round the room. One of the dressing table drawers was on the floor but the wardrobe was the only piece of furniture out of place.

"There were two of them." He sounded bitter. "They came in through the doors."

Antony had good reason to be resentful, he'd seen a lot of money disappear down the garden path tonight. "Dear, dear. Well, I did warn you to check that repair job didn't I?"

"Victoria!" April was understandably bewildered by my callous tone. I was feeling a lot more than callous, however — the way I felt about Antony a handful of salt would have come in useful.

She stood up and gave me an exasperated look. "I'd better go and tell Debs we're okay, and I'll ring an ambulance for Antony."

I was about to say Antony could bloody well walk to casualty but she was already on her way. Wandering over to the wardrobe I peered into the fist-sized hole that had been punched through the back. "You know, my guess is that your visitors found you'd got there first."

"What are you talking about?" He was shakily on his feet, stepping into a pair of underpants. From the beads of sweat on his forehead it looked as if the process was hurting him a lot. Good, I was pleased.

"Why did they do that to your back if they weren't after some information? I think they broke in, found you here and told you to keep quiet." I was improvising but it sounded right. "They did a little furniture moving and discovered you'd got there already ... Yes?"

He was panting with the effort but was now halfway into a pair of jeans. As he pulled the zip up his face mouth contorted in pain. Above it, however, his eyes were rat-like and cunning, and not pretty at all.

I bent over the drawer on the floor. "My God, now what could they have been rifling through your designer knickers for?" Crouching down I studied a faint trace of white powder in a corner. "Not talcum surely?" I dabbed my finger and gave an appreciative sniff, just so he knew that I knew.

"You interfering bitch." He lurched menacingly across the room. "Get out of there!" Despite his back problem Antony was a lot bigger than I and from where I was sitting it rather looked as if his right foot was about to launch itself into my face.

I feinted. "Don't even think about it."

Antony didn't know it at the time but he was in the process of making a life decision. If he'd touched me I wouldn't have gone along with April later. I have a weakness for revenge. He hesitated, thought better of it — after all the police were about to make an entrance — then turned and ran out into the hall. I jumped up after him, caught my foot in the rucked brown carpet, and as I fell hit my head on the bookcase.

It was a good thing April had called that ambulance after all.

CHAPTER TWENTY-FOUR

The sound is like the rustle of long linen skirts across grass . . .

"April?"

There's a hand on the pillow near my head, but I don't recognize the cheery voice that answers. "Almost! It's early May so you're not far out. Don't worry, it's only to be expected, you've had a nasty knock on the head."

She's wearing something white, and a cap. A nurse. I try to lift my head as she walks away but a hot wave of pain shooting from the base of my skull and slamming into my right eye soon puts a stop to that. I've seen enough, however, to tell me this is a hospital.

"The quieter you keep the better. Drink this and get some more sleep." A trickle of water runs down my chin. And then all of a sudden I'm dancing, I'm dancing with April who's wearing bright red shoes and we're part of a large circle of women, a circle of women dancing and holding hands.

EPILOGUE

The sky was blue, the blue of forget-me-nots, the blue of birds' eggs ... Almost the blue of a policeman's uniform, and I'd seen more than one of those over the past couple of days.

April, Phoebe and I were lying out on the quad. We'd had lunch in Hall and April was discussing a visit she was making later in the day to Deborah's hairdresser, where she intended to have most of her hair cut off. My own had been styled by the hospital around an egg-shaped lump and an impressive collection of stitches.

"Do you think it will suit me short?" she asked.

"It'll be summer soon, you'll like feeling cool."

April could shave her hair off and I wouldn't mind at all, I'd got past the stage of loving her simply for the length of her hair or the color of her eyes. Which weren't blue today, I noticed, but grey.

"When is Eleanor coming down for you?" Phoebe asked.

"Oh, sometime soon, she said it won't take long."

"Maybe Bernard's going to give you a medal." April fondly pushed against my right foot with hers.

"I doubt that somehow." The winter pansies had vanished from the window boxes and in their place lilies of the valley nodded graceful heads. May, the white month, lilies, cherry blossoms ...

"And so when does Antony begin his new job?" Phoebe rolled onto her stomach and propped herself up on her elbows.

"Don't ask me, I'm not the dispenser of justice around here." I sat up gingerly, in case my head felt obliged to start pounding again, and brushed grass cuttings off my skirt.

April said, "He starts first thing next Monday and if he sticks out the year College will consider having him back."

"And if he doesn't?" Phoebe asked her.

"There are ways of making sure he doesn't get into higher education anywhere else. Antony knows he needs a degree, and his parents seem pretty determined that this attempt at reform will work."

"A voluntary worker for an AIDS charity, I like it!" Phoebe chuckled.

"All April's doing I'll have you know. She came up with the suggestion that we needn't tell the police he was responsible for the letters, or that he knew about the drugs, and Eleanor and Rosemary got Bernard to agree to this trial year. Bernard wasn't averse to the idea on the grounds that it would at least keep the name of one more student out of the papers."

April sat up too. "Victoria doesn't think a year's good works will turn Antony into a decent human being and she's undoubtedly right, but at least he'll be doing something useful. Six months inside would only make him worse. And I don't like to think of what might happen to him in jail, anyway. I wouldn't want that on my conscience."

I loved April for her conscience. And for the way she was rubbing my toes in public.

"I think we all know what would happen to a pretty boy like that," Phoebe responded. "Do you think they'll catch the men who killed Erich?"

"I don't know," I said, "but there must have been quite a stash hidden in that wardrobe. Antony was bloody lucky they only indulged in some mild torture. He genuinely seems to have had no idea of the danger he was putting himself in when he moved into April's room. He appears to have convinced himself that Erich's murder was pure coincidence."

"That's what I call thick."

"Greedy is what I call it."

Across the other side of the quad two boys wearing loud shirts were joined by a group of young women whose tans let you know they'd been able to afford Easter abroad. One of them, a redhead with a skirt that revealed remarkably long legs, smiled across at April. The message was loud and clear, she was looking good and didn't care who else knew it. It was also clear that she rather liked what she was looking at. April smiled back.

"O love, Lay on thy whips": monogamy wasn't something we'd ever discussed, which was remiss of me, I usually like to make sure at the start that everyone's agreed on the ground rules.

Phoebe checked her watch. "The punt's booked for two o'clock. Malcolm said he'd meet us there. I should warn you now that he'll bring lager so we'd better get some decent wine on the way."

"I like lager," I said.

"You're joking I hope." April's attention came back to me. I wasn't, but now Eleanor was walking slowly towards us.

Rosemary gestured for me to take the leather armchair between hers and Eleanor's under the window. She gave a warm smile but she was looking tired. In the past few days she'd been looking older as well, but then we probably all had. Bernard was lodged behind his desk, studiously avoiding my eyes.

The story they had to tell wasn't particularly unusual.

"How many cheques have been used?" I asked.

"Five." Bernard's voice was clipped. "The Treasurer couldn't even see where they'd been in the book at first, he had to search."

"They would have been cut out with a razor."

He looked bewildered that I'd know something like that.

"And you say about three thousand pounds has gone from this account?"

"Yes." Eleanor was quiet but businesslike. "We don't know who's responsible. Of course it's most likely to be one of the accounts office staff, but ..."

But it could be one of them, a member of the Senior Common Room, someone they'd just been rubbing elbows with at High Table.

"We are anxious," Bernard was saying, "that this matter be treated with the utmost confidence, Ms. Cross ..."

Ms. Cross, get that, Bernard was trying hard. Drugs, murder, now this: that knighthood was getting more remote by the minute.

I explained that I couldn't take this job on privately but only through the agency. Bernard wasn't thrilled by the news; however there wasn't much he could do about it. We agreed on rates and I warned them that I couldn't promise to recover their funds but I could at least make some suggestions about how to avoid this sort of thing happening in future.

As I got up to leave I turned and looked out the window: below, against the emerald grass, April's dress was a splash of white. She was looking up in my direction and I leaned past Rosemary to give her a wide wave.

I'd been wrong about summer being just around the corner, it was already here.

Also of interest:

Mary Wings
Divine Victim

From the author of the bestselling *She Came Too Late* and *She Came in a Flash*.

Marya inherits a bucketload of money and a creepy old house in desolate Montana. But she has to live in it for a year if she wants to claim the cash, and persuading her lover to stay there with her is more than a little tricky. Soon the two women are embroiled in mystery as their own past secrets, and the secrets of the house, are gradually uncovered, until the tension builds to a fierce double climax that few could have foreseen . . .

'Wings has managed to plug directly into the thriller mainstream without compromising her sexuality or politics.'

John Conquest, *Time Out*

Crime fiction   £5.99
ISBN 0 7043 4323 1

Mary Wings
She Came Too Late
She Came in a Flash

Emma Victor, intrepid lesbian detective, in two earth-shaking murder mysteries. Too late to save the victims from their untimely deaths, she battles to establish the identity of the murderers, as the action threatens to reach explosion point . . .

About: She Came Too Late

'A quick, exciting and sophisticated thriller.' *Guardian*

Crime fiction   £4.95
ISBN 0 7043 3995 1

About: She Came in a Flash

'Moves along at a very good pace to a surprising but tough finish. Recommended.' *Canberra Times*

Crime fiction   £4.95
ISBN 0 7043 4108 5

Deborah Powell
Bayou City Secrets
Houston Town

Blunt-talking investigative reporter Hollis Carpenter in two
dangerous and deadly mysteries. In the tough, hard-paced
world of Prohibition America, only the beautiful Lily might
help ease the pain . . .

'Lots of exciting hard-boiled fun, with Hollis never far from a
wisecrack.'   *Reading for Pleasure*

'A new mystery yarn by Deborah Powell is to classic
gumshoe dramas what Dom Pérignon is to champagne . . .
one of the best.'   *The Washington Blade*

'fast-moving, entertaining'   *Publishers Weekly*

Bayou City Secrets
Crime fiction   £5.99
ISBN 0 7043 4326 6

Houston Town
Crime fiction   £5.99
ISBN 0 7043 4327 4

Marcia Muller
Pennies on a Dead Woman's Eyes

Sharon McCone, PI, returns, this time to prove the innocence of a woman convicted of murder, many years before. Now, in a race against the clock and with a list full of suspects, McCone herself becomes a target amidst escalating violence.

'Muller's dense plots are models of construction.'
New York Times Book Review

'McCone is one of the most freshly conceived and complexly characterized of the female private eyes.' *Publishers Weekly*

Crime fiction   £5.99
ISBN 0 7043 4337 1

Marcia Muller
Trophies and Dead Things

Sharon McCone, private eye, must now investigate a series
of seemingly random murders. And then they start to strike
surprisingly close to home . . .

'Muller and her investigator, Sharon McCone, hit top form.'
Booklist

'*Trophies and Dead Things* is, above all, compelling.'
Newsweek

'One of Muller's best.' *Kirkus Reviews*

Crime fiction   £5.99
ISBN 0 7043 4314 2

Marcia Muller
Where Echoes Live

Residents around Tufa Lake are resisting the reopening of a
gold mine. And then a body is discovered. Enter Sharon
McCone . . .

'Muller produces the sort of thrillers that enthusiasts always
hope for, but rarely get.'   *The Sunday Times*

'Muller's pace and plotting are very strong, but it's her
characters – especially McCone – who will lure you back.'
                                        Atlanta Journal-Constitution

Crime fiction   £5.99
ISBN 0 7043 4315 0